"They think I have something to do with it," Felicity said, her voice so quiet Gage almost couldn't make out the words. **"I can tell."**

"No. You've been through this before. You know how it goes." He found a loaf of bread and dropped a slice in the toaster. "They have questions they have to ask just to make sure, but—"

"It's the second time." She lifted her gaze to meet his, and there was nothing timid or uncertain about her like there had been in the past. No, she was in complete control, even lost and scared. "The questions were different. And they're right. It does. It has something to do with me. I know it does."

BACKCOUNTRY ESCAPE

Nicole Helm

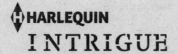

For the helpers.

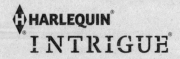

HARLEQUIN®
INTRIGUE®

ISBN-13: 978-1-335-13648-0

Recycling programs
for this product may
not exist in your area.

Backcountry Escape

Copyright © 2020 by Nicole Helm

All rights reserved. No part of this book may be used or reproduced in
any manner whatsoever without written permission except in the case of
brief quotations embodied in critical articles and reviews.

This is a work of fiction. Names, characters, places and incidents
are either the product of the author's imagination or are used fictitiously.
Any resemblance to actual persons, living or dead, businesses,
companies, events or locales is entirely coincidental.

This edition published by arrangement with Harlequin Books S.A.

For questions and comments about the quality of this book,
please contact us at CustomerService@Harlequin.com.

Harlequin Enterprises ULC
22 Adelaide St. West, 40th Floor
Toronto, Ontario M5H 4E3, Canada
www.Harlequin.com

Printed in U.S.A.

Nicole Helm grew up with her nose in a book and the dream of one day becoming a writer. Luckily, after a few failed career choices, she gets to follow that dream—writing down-to-earth contemporary romance and romantic suspense. From farmers to cowboys, Midwest to *the* West, Nicole writes stories about people finding themselves and finding love in the process. She lives in Missouri with her husband and two sons and dreams of someday owning a barn.

Visit the Author Profile page at Harlequin.com.

CAST OF CHARACTERS

Gage Wyatt—Wyatt brother, twin to Brady. Sheriff's deputy in Valiant County, South Dakota. Crush on Felicity.

Felicity Harrison—Park ranger at Badlands National Park. One of Duke Knight's foster girls. Crush on Brady Wyatt.

Brady Wyatt—Gage's twin brother. Also a sheriff's deputy. More serious twin.

Ace Wyatt—The Wyatt brothers' father. A dangerous biker gang president. Currently in jail.

Grandma Pauline Reaves—The Wyatt brothers' grandmother who took them in after they escaped their father's gang.

Michael Harrison—Felicity's biological father. She was taken away from him as a child because he was abusive.

Rachel Knight—Felicity's foster sister who lives at the Knight ranch.

Liza Dean-Wyatt—Felicity's foster sister, married to the oldest Wyatt brother. Takes care of young half sister, Gigi.

Jamison Wyatt—The oldest Wyatt brother.

Cody Wyatt—Youngest Wyatt brother, married to Nina, father to Brianna.

Chapter One

Felicity Harrison had learned two things since coming to live with Duke and Eva Knight when she'd been just four years old, with a broken arm and black eye courtesy of her father.

First, she loved the outdoors. She could hike for days and sleep under the stars every night given the chance. Didn't matter the season or the weather. In her mind the winds of the South Dakota Badlands had made her, and she was part of that stark, awe-inspiring landscape.

The second thing had taken her a little longer to figure out, but once she'd hit puberty she'd been sure.

She was desperately, irrevocably in love with Brady Wyatt.

Despite the fact she was nearing thirty and he'd never shown any interest in her that he didn't show all of her foster sisters, Felicity hadn't fully given up on the prospect that Brady might notice her at some point.

It was possible. She had made changes in her life the past few years. Between her epic shyness and intermittent stutter, high school and college had been a bit of a disaster but she'd found her passion in parks and recreation—as much as people would laugh at her zeal for nature.

In finding her passion at an early age, and making it her career, parks and rec had ended up being the thing that gave her some confidence. The drive to succeed had helped—or maybe forced—her to overcome some of her issues and bumps in the road.

After years of seasonal work in the national park system, she'd finally landed her dream job as a park ranger at Badlands National Park, her home. The job had been hard and challenging, and it had *changed her*.

She wasn't the same Felicity she'd been.

Brady hadn't noticed yet because he was so busy. Being a police officer and EMT in Valiant County took up a lot of his time. Plus, he lived a good hour away and spent free time at his grandmother's ranch even farther out.

She just needed the opportunity to show him who she'd become, and *surely* he'd fall for her the way she'd fallen for him all those years ago.

She daydreamed about that opportunity while she took her normal morning hike. Summer was inching its way into the mornings so she didn't need her park jacket over her sweatshirt. It was her favorite time of year, and that put a smile on her face and pep in her step.

The sky was a moody gray. Likely they'd have storms by afternoon, but she imagined the sky was a bright summer blue and Brady was hiking with her. He'd hold her hand and they'd talk about what birds they were hearing.

Her fantasies about Brady were always just like that.

Soft, sweet, relaxing. Brady was steady. Calm. His five brothers were wilder or edgier, even Jamison. As the oldest, Jamison was serious, and seriously noble, but there was a sharpness to him that had taken Felicity time to grow accustomed to.

But Brady? He was even-keeled. He didn't shout or swear. He believed in right and wrong, and he appreciated the importance of his duties as an EMT. He took care of people. *Healed* people.

Calm and good and healing were definitely things she wanted in her life.

She was so caught up in her fantasy she almost tripped over the boot in the middle of the path.

She regained her footing and looked down at the brown boot. It was unlaced, and the soles were caked with dirt.

Felicity stared at it as the slow roll of cold shock spread out through her body. For a second her vision blurred and sound disappeared. She couldn't suck in a breath. She could only stand and look at the boot.

She'd seen this before, done this before. It was happening again.

No.

Her mind rejected the possibility and she managed to breathe in, let it slowly out. It was just a boot. People lost weird things on the trail all the time. Maybe it had gotten too heavy. Maybe it was broken.

There were a million reasons. A million. Besides, it wasn't even the same kind of boot as…the last time. This one was clearly a woman's, if the bright pink laces were anything to go by. It was an accident. A coincidence.

You have to check.

She nodded to herself as if that would make her move. Make this okay. As if she could will away all the similarities to last year.

There wouldn't be a body this time. Couldn't be.

Just keep walking.

You can't just keep walking!

Her mind turned over and over, reminding herself of a Felicity she didn't like very much. She stepped purposefully away from the boot. It wouldn't be like last year. She would turn to the right and look off the path. She would see nothing but rocks and the stray scrubby flora.

First she looked left. Because…because she had to work up to it. There was nothing but mixed grass prairie that existed on that side of the trail. It was fine.

The right side was where the last body had been. There wouldn't be one. There *couldn't* be one. She forced herself to turn, to take the few steps to the very edge of the trail.

This side was rock, geological deposits that brought people to the Badlands in droves every summer. There wouldn't be a body. Couldn't be.

But there was.

She stared at the mess of limbs all at wrong angles. She stared, frozen, willing the image to disappear. The canyon to the side of the trail was narrow and deep, but you'd have to be sincerely not paying attention to fall down it, or…

Or.

She finally managed to squeeze her eyes shut, last year's memories rushing back like a movie in her head.

Unseeing eyes and a black beard then. Now, a woman facedown in the rock, hair moving in the wind.

Nausea rolled through her, but she swallowed it down and tried to think. Tried to remember where and what she was.

Don't touch anything. Don't touch. Don't touch.

She took a few stumbling steps back on the trail.

Last time, she'd checked the body with a thought to help. Last time, she'd compromised the crime scene trying to identify the person while waiting for the cops. Last time, she'd made so many mistakes.

Not this time.

She nodded to herself again. This time she'd do it right. Not mess with anything. Not ruin anything.

How could it be *happening again*?

"One step at a time, Felicity. One step at a time."

She was calmed by the sound of her own voice, even if there was no one around she was talking to. She pulled out her phone, called the local police department and radioed her boss so he could get someone out to seal off the area.

Then she called Brady. She couldn't help it. When she was in trouble—when she or any of her foster sisters were in trouble—they always turned to the Wyatt boys.

They always came, and they always helped. Because they were good men, and Brady was the best of them, in her estimation.

When he answered, she managed to tell him what had happened, though she felt detached and as if she was speaking through dense fog. He promised she wouldn't have to be alone.

She tried to allow that reassurance to soothe her, but mostly she settled in to wait, hoping she wouldn't throw up.

"SHE CALLED *YOU*," Gage Wyatt grumbled at his brother through the phone receiver tucked between his ear and shoulder as he navigated the highway in front of him.

Summer had turned the hills green, and the tall grass waved in the wind. Gage had always gotten a kick out of the fact that's exactly what his ancestors would have seen when they'd arrived here by cart and horse.

He couldn't find amusement today as his twin brother tasked him with something he most especially did not want to do.

"I can't make it," Brady lectured. "I called Tuck, but he didn't answer. He's likely on a case. You're closer than Jamison, Cody and Dev—not that I'd send Dev. She needs someone there ASAP, Gage."

Gage swore inwardly, not sure how out of the six Wyatt brothers he was the *only* one available. He kept his voice light and offhanded, the Gage Wyatt special. "She's moon-eyed over you. That's why she called *you*."

There was only the briefest of pauses in return. "She found a body." Brady's tone was flat, the kind of flat his voice got when no amount of coaxing, arguing or nonchalance was going to irritate him into caving. "Another body."

"All right, all right," Gage muttered. "I'm not too far

off." At least in the grand scheme of things in South Dakota. An hour, tops. "Same place?"

"No." Brady related where exactly in the park Felicity had stumbled across a body. Not too far from her park ranger cabin.

She'd found *another* body. The same thing had happened to Felicity last year, and it was horrible, to say the least, that she was dealing with that again. Gage listened as Brady explained where he'd need to go to get to Felicity. He turned his truck around and started heading for the park while Brady spoke.

"Be gentle with her," Brady said. "You know Felicity."

"Yeah." He did, he thought grimly as he hung up and tossed his cell phone onto the passenger seat. He knew her better than his brother did apparently.

Felicity wasn't the same shy wallflower she'd been growing up. Ever since she'd gotten that job at Badlands and moved home—well, closer to home—she'd been more sure of herself, more…something. He didn't like to dwell on that considering she was so hung up on Brady.

Who apparently didn't even notice she'd grown up, no matter how long it had taken her.

She'd held up really well last year when she'd found the body. It had seemed like a freak accident, and she had seemed able to handle it, especially admirable since she wasn't used to dealing with dead bodies. As a police officer, he had dealt with quite a few, not always violent or tragic. Sometimes as simple as someone going to sleep and not waking up.

It was part of the job, and even if it wasn't, he'd grown up in a biker gang until his oldest brother had gotten him and Brady out when they'd been eleven. He'd seen worse there living among the Sons of the Badlands those eleven years, especially considering his father ran the group. Ace Wyatt didn't deal in mercy—he dealt in his own warped version of justice.

Thanks to his oldest brother, Jamison, Gage had never believed in his father's justice. But he'd had to survive it, and the body count, before he'd had the maturity or the badge to cope with it.

Now he had both, but no matter how much Felicity had come into her own lately, she wasn't supposed to have to deal with dead bodies.

Plural. The pattern here made him uneasy. It was rare park rangers found bodies when not part of a search for missing people. Rarer still to have it happen to the same ranger twice.

She did need someone, but Gage didn't know why Brady hadn't called one of her foster sisters. Most of them would do better with the whole soothing and reassuring task ahead of him.

Likely Brady had called him because he knew some of the police officers with Pennington County, and none of the Knight fosters would. They might soothe, but Gage would be able to get some answers.

Gage would get those answers for Felicity. It was the soothing and reassuring part he wasn't so keen on. He tended to keep a hands-off policy as much as possible when it came to her.

"Grown woman," Gage muttered to himself, tapping his agitated fingers against the wheel as he drove. "Did this before. She'll do it again."

He pressed the gas pedal a little hard.

"Didn't she just help save Cody and Nina's butts?" he demanded in an imaginary argument with Brady. "She's capable. More than." Wasn't that half the reason he kept his distance? Capable Felicity in love with his twin brother was dangerous to his well-being.

He muttered to himself on the long, empty drive to the Badlands. Usually he'd marvel at the scenery. Even living here his whole life, he didn't take for granted the rolling grassland that turned into buttes and the grand rock formations that made up the park and its surrounding areas. But he was working up a good irritated steam—mostly as a defense mechanism against Felicity in particular.

She *was* moon-eyed over Brady. So it made sense that since she'd grown a spine and begun showing it off, Gage had started having a little more than friendly thoughts about her. What didn't make sense was harboring those more-than-friendly feelings knowing full well she worshipped the ground Brady walked on.

Who could blame her? His brothers were saints as far as he was concerned. Oh, Cody and Dev had a bit of an edge to them, but at the heart of it they were all good men.

Then there was Brady, something better than a good man. Smartest of all of them, honorable without being hard about it. By the book and serious, yet affable enough that everyone *loved* Brady. He never said the wrong thing, never offered an inappropriate joke to ease the tension. If all his brothers were saints, Brady was the king saint.

On the other hand Gage was the one who said the wrong thing for a laugh. Who didn't take anything as earnestly as his brothers took their breakfast choices.

Of *course* Felicity had a thing for Brady, and it seemed inevitable that Gage had the bad luck to be hung up on someone in love with his perfect twin.

He rolled his shoulders as he pulled into the parking lot for the trail Felicity had been hiking. This wasn't about him, his issues or even his stupid feelings.

This was about Felicity. Helping her with a sad co-incidence. Coming across her second dead body in as many years.

He ignored a tingly *this is all wrong* feeling between his shoulder blades and flashed a broad grin to the cop stationed at the blocked-off trailhead.

He pulled out his badge, did some sweet-talking and was heading toward Felicity in a few minutes.

Once he reached the area where the cops and park rangers were huddled, he stopped short and took a min-ute to observe Felicity. She sat on a rock away from the circle of people. She was deathly pale, her fingers twisted together, and she stared hard at them.

His heart ached, very much against his will. As a sheriff's deputy for Valiant County, he'd dealt with his share of victims and innocent bystanders of awful things. He knew how to deal with the walking wounded.

But he actually *knew* Felicity, and had since he'd escaped to Grandma's ranch. He'd been eleven to her nine. He'd witnessed her nearly mute elementary years, an awkward-at-best adolescence and then eventually this change in her. Now, in front of him sat a woman who was not falling apart though she had every right to.

That twisting feeling dug deeper so he pushed himself forward. "Hey."

She looked up slowly, her eyebrows drawing together in dawning confusion. "I called Brady."

The twist grew teeth, and he might have grinned negligently in a different situation. But she'd just found a body, so Gage shrugged instead and didn't let the burn of her disappointment settle inside of him. "He sent me. I was closest."

She stared at him for a few seconds before she finally jerked her chin in some approximation of a nod. "They already—" she swallowed, a slight tremor going through her body "—moved the body out."

"Any ID?"

Felicity shook her head. "Nothing on her."

"Her. So, this is different than…" He winced at how insensitive he sounded. Sure, it worked when you were a cop. Not so much when you were here as a friend.

She paused. "Yes," she said finally, in a way that was not convincing at all. "Different."

"Let's get you back to your place, huh?"

She gestured helplessly at the team of cops and park officials. "I have to…"

"They know where to find you if they need more information. Come on. You probably haven't eaten since breakfast." He pulled her to her feet and easily slid his arm around her shoulders since he knew she'd balk at moving if he didn't give her a physical push.

She smelled like flowers and summer. Quite the opposite of the situation they were dealing with.

She pressed a hand to her stomach, her heels all but digging in where she stood. "I couldn't eat. I can't."

"We'll see. You want to walk back?"

She looked around, dismay clear as day on her face. "No, but I need to."

He understood that. If she didn't walk back the way she'd come, she'd be afraid of returning this way even when her job necessitated it.

Still, he had to give her a push, and he tried not to feel a bit sick over the fact he was forcing her to do something she didn't want to do. Even if she needed to. He followed the trail back toward her cabin, keeping a tight grip on her shoulders as they walked.

A cold drizzle began to fall, but neither of them commented on it or hurried their pace. It felt like a slow trudge through chilled molasses, and Gage didn't have the heart to speed her up even as she began to shiver.

When they got to the authorized-user-only trail, Gage took it without qualm. It would lead to her park housing, and he'd get some food in her. Encourage her to rest.

Then, when she wasn't so pale, he'd head back to the ranch. Felicity wouldn't want him to stay anyway. She'd either handle it on her own, or he'd call one of her sisters for her.

Her little cabin was situated in a small grove of trees. It was old, but she'd infused it with a kind of hominess, though he couldn't identify how. Just that it looked like a nice place.

He reached the door and waited for her to pull out her keys. She unlocked the door and stepped inside.

He'd hoped the walk would have helped put some color back in her cheeks, but she still looked pale as death and like a stray wind might knock her over. Her red hair was damp, and the tendrils that had escaped her braid stuck to her ashen skin.

"Go change into something dry."

She looked up at him, her green eyes lost and sad. She didn't say anything, just stood there looking at him.

"Go on. I'll fix you something to eat while you change."

She shook her head. "I'll just throw it up."

"We'll see. Go on now." He shooed her toward where he figured her bedroom was, down a short, narrow hallway.

He went to the cramped kitchen and poked around for something to make that would go down easy. He found an unreasonable amount of tea and picked one that looked particularly soothing. He followed the instructions, trying not to feel claustrophobic in her closet of a kitchen.

When she returned she didn't look any less lost, but she was in dry sweatpants and a long-sleeved T-shirt for Mammoth Cave National Park. She stood at the entrance to the kitchen taking in her surroundings like it was somewhere she'd never been before.

"Sit," he ordered, uncomfortable with how fragile she seemed.

She nodded after a time and then took a seat at her tiny table. He set the mug of tea in front of her. "You'll drink all of that," he said, trying to sound as commanding as his grandmother did when she was forcing food on someone.

She didn't drink, just stared at the mug. "They think I have something to do with it," she said, her voice so quiet he almost couldn't make out the words. "I can tell."

"No. You've been through this before. You know how it goes." He found a loaf of bread and dropped a slice in the toaster. "They have questions they have to ask just to make sure, but—"

"It's the second time." She lifted her gaze to meet his, and there was nothing timid or uncertain about her, as there had been in the past. No, she was in complete control, even lost and scared. "The questions were different. And they're right. It does. It has something to do with me. I know it does."

Chapter Two

Something about Gage's large form taking up almost the entire space in her tiny kitchen made Felicity want to blurt out everything that was going on in her brain.

He was making her tea and toast. She wanted to lay down her head and cry. She expected her sisters to take care of her. She even expected Duke to take care of her—he'd had to step in as mother along with father when Eva had died. He'd done his best.

Her foster family had always done their best, just like their friends the Wyatts.

But this was Gage. Gage always made her feel edgy. Like she was on uneven ground. You never knew what Gage was going to do or say, and she preferred knowing exactly what was going to happen.

Sometimes she blamed his size for the discomfort she felt. He was so tall and broad and, Lord, he packed on the muscle. But Brady was the exact same size, just as strong and broad, and Brady only ever made her feel safe. Comfortable.

Gage set down a plate with a piece of buttered toast

in front of her. Her cheap, cute floral dishes looked all wrong in his hands.

Today was all, *all* wrong.

"Why do you think it has something to do with you?" he asked as he took a seat across from her.

"You made me tea and toast." She could only stare at the wisps of steam drifting up from the mug. Gage Wyatt…had made her tea and toast?

"You're lucky. If Grandma Pauline was here, she would have made a five-course meal and insisted you eat every bite."

It was true. His grandmother soothed with food—whether you wanted food as soothing or not. Tea and toast was a lighter option, and her stomach might actually be able to handle it. So she sipped the tea, took a bite of toast and avoided the topic of conversation at hand.

"Felicity."

She winced at the gentleness in his tone. "Why did Brady send you?" She squeezed her eyes shut. "I'm sorry. That sounds ungrateful."

He shrugged again, just as he had outside when she'd made a point of telling him he wasn't who she'd been expecting. There was something in his gaze when he gave those careless shrugs that made her heart feel weighted. Like she'd said something all wrong and hurt his feelings.

Which was ludicrous. Gage did not get hurt feelings, especially at her hands.

"Like I said outside, I was closest." He tapped his fingers on the table, the only sign of agitation.

"You've been very…nice," she said, not even sure why she wanted to try to make him feel better when any hurt or agitation had to be her imagination.

"I'm always nice."

"No. That is not true. Not that you're mean, but I'm not sure anyone would describe you as nice." Gage was challenging. He was irreverent. He made her jumpy. Even when he was doing something nice.

"Felicity. Why do you think this crime connects to you?"

The toast turned to lead in her throat and she had to work to swallow it down. She didn't want to talk about it, but she needed to. She needed help. From someone in law enforcement who would listen to her. "It was the same."

"A woman this time," he noted. "So, not exactly the same."

"Maybe not the *who*, but it was my morning hike. My routine. I've changed it a little since last year, but I always have a routine." Routine steadied her. Made her feel strong and in control, and now she wasn't sure she'd be able to have one or feel that ever again. "The last time, it was my routine hike. My personal routine hike—not work related. Just like this time."

He nodded and waited patiently for her to work up to say the rest of it.

"The boot in the trail. Unlaced. That happened last time, too. I stumbled over the boot last time. This time I saw it in the nick of time—probably the pink laces." Those laces would haunt her forever.

"Okay. So you saw the boot, and then what?"

She'd already told the Pennington County deputies and her boss the answer to that question. Over and over in a circle. But she hadn't explained to them what she was about to explain to Gage. "I told them I looked on the sides of the trail to see if anyone had had an accident."

"You told them…"

"I knew where the body would be. I looked on the left side first because that wasn't where the body was last time. I looked to the left and there was no one there, but I had to check. It would be on the right side of the trail. I didn't want there to be, but I just… I just knew the body would be where it had been last time. Only a few feet off the trail." She shoved away the tea and the toast and got to her feet. "I can't…"

There was nowhere to go in her tiny cabin. Stomp off to her room like a child? Tempting.

But Gage walked right over to her, putting his big hands on her shoulders and squeezing them enough to center her in the moment.

He was so dang tall, and it was unreasonable how broad-shouldered he was. When he was clean-shaven, he looked so much like Brady it got hard to tell them apart. But their eyes were different. Brady's hazel edged toward brown, and Gage's green. Gage's nose was crooked, and he had a scar through his eyebrow.

Brady's face was perfect. Gage's was…

"You know, Brady told me I needed to be gentle with you."

Those words felt like cold water being splashed in her face. "I'm not a shy little girl anymore," she snapped, trying to shrug off his hands. When would they all see that? It wasn't enough she'd helped save Cody and Nina from one of the Sons last month? Honestly.

"That's what I told him," Gage said, which had her looking up in confusion.

"You…"

"Anyone who's paying attention can see you've changed, Felicity. You're an adult. You've found yourself or whatever you want to call it."

Did that mean *Gage* was paying attention? Impossible.

"Now. You've done this before. So, don't say you can't when we both know you can and you will."

She sucked in a breath. He was right. It didn't quite steady her, though. Why was Gage of all people right? And why were his big hands on her narrow shoulders?

As if he'd read her thoughts, his hands slid away and he stepped back, shoving his hands into his pockets.

"Why couldn't it be random? I mean, it looks like the killings connect. It's not accidental and it's not suicide. It's murder—even I could see that no matter how much they tried to BS me. But just because it's murder, doesn't mean you're the key. Maybe Badlands is the common denominator. Maybe you're just…"

"Unlucky?"

"Sure. Why not? The bodies aren't showing up on your doorstep."

"Just on trails I walk as a matter of course," she returned, wishing she could believe his coincidence theory. "That boot wasn't an accident, and it wasn't placed there yesterday when anyone could have come across it. It was put there so *I* would come across it."

"Okay." He nodded, taking a few more steps away from her.

It seemed odd, the forced distance, but she could hardly think about anything going on with Gage when she had a dead body to worry about.

"If you're being targeted…why?"

"I don't know." She didn't have a clue. Maybe she'd believe it was her connection to the Wyatts. She'd shot one of the Sons of the Badlands men to help Nina and Cody escape Ace Wyatt's machinations. Except she'd never had a personal interaction with Ace Wyatt, the president of the gang and Gage's father, who was now in jail.

But jail hadn't stopped Ace from making things happen on the outside last month. Why would she think he couldn't reach her now?

The problem was that last month was the first time she'd ever interfered with Sons business, which didn't explain the first body from a year ago.

Unless that *had* been an accident and this was a copycat?

"You think it's Ace."

Felicity looked up at Gage because his voice was so flat. Even when Gage got angry he usually hid it under that natural irreverence. It was why she preferred Brady. Brady was rather stoic, but when he showed an emotion you knew what emotion you were getting. Gage was unpredictable.

Even now. She didn't know what that cold, flat voice

meant. She only knew it was possible this connected to his crime boss of a father, even if Ace was in jail and the Sons of the Badlands seemed to be getting weaker.

"I don't know. I don't know, but I interfered last month."

"It wouldn't connect all the way back to last year." He kept talking before she could offer her theory. "But it wouldn't have to—it would just have to look like it. Sounds like Ace."

She nodded. "I need you to help me figure out if it is, Gage. I can't trust the local police to do it. I'm sure they're fine at their jobs, but they don't know Ace, and they're afraid of the Sons. You aren't."

"Everyone is afraid of the Sons, Felicity. It's stupid not to be." He sighed, presumably at the horrified look on her face. "We'll figure it out. Okay?"

SHE WAS STANDING still as a statue, looking at him like he'd slapped her across the face when he'd simply told her the truth.

Even if the Sons were weaker than they'd been, they were still dangerous. Too dangerous, and anyone with a connection to Ace Wyatt was definitely in the most danger.

They were working on getting more charges leveled against Ace, thanks to three of the men who had been arrested after trying to hurt Cody and Nina and their daughter last month. But it still wouldn't add up to a life sentence, even if he was found guilty at his upcoming trial for the first round of charges.

Unfortunately, no matter how sure Jamison and

Cody were that the law would keep Ace powerless—when Ace had already proved jail couldn't—Gage had doubts.

Major doubts.

Felicity *had* been integral in the arrest of one of those men who was potentially going to take the stand against Ace. It made sense she'd be targeted.

Gage's phone chimed and he looked down at the text from Brady.

I can relieve you if you want.

Felicity would want Brady. She deserved the Wyatt brother she preferred even if her crush was hopeless. Brady didn't have a clue who Felicity really was. Gage wasn't convinced his twin could ever look at the Knight fosters and not see a *sister*. Or at the least think, *Hands off.*

Brady would always toe the unofficial line. Gage never did.

No worries, he typed and hit Send before he could talk himself into doing the right thing.

Maybe Felicity wanted Brady, but Gage would be the better helper in this situation. He was willing to bend a few more rules than Brady. Besides, she'd said she needed *his* help. Maybe it was only because he was here, but hell, he was here.

"Once they ID her, we'll want to see how she connects to the first victim."

Felicity shook her head and took a seat. "I don't think the victims matter. I mean, they matter. To their families. To me. But they're not the point to whoever is doing this."

"Maybe not, but we'll research it all the same. We'll go over things. Maybe you should stay at the ranch until this blows over."

She was shaking her head. "I have a job to do. If I run away from that—"

"They're going to put you on leave. They did last time, didn't they?"

"They can't. It's summer this time. It's busy season. I'm scheduled for programs and…" She trailed off as her phone buzzed. She swallowed and looked at the screen. "It's my boss."

Gage didn't say *I told you so*. He didn't need to. Didn't want to after having to stand and listen to her desperate attempts to change her boss's mind.

When she finally hung up, she stared at her phone. "I can't work for at least a week."

"That's not such a bad thing."

Her head whipped up, fury in her green eyes. "It's a terrible thing. On every level. I can't *be* here. It will haunt me—her body. Every night. You can't get rid of something you never face. It puts my job, my *dream* job, in jeopardy. Do you have any idea how hard I've worked to get this position?"

The color had come back to her face, the faintest blush rising in her cheeks. She was breathing a little heavier after that tirade, and she had her fingers curled into fists.

She was possibly the most beautiful woman he'd

ever seen, and he knew that made him a jerk. "Yeah," he finally managed. "You worked your butt off."

His simple affirmative had her slumping in her seat. "I don't want to go to the ranch. Duke will worry. Sarah and Rachel will worry and fuss. Your grandmother will make a feast for seventy and expect a handful of us to eat it all. Worst of all, you Wyatt boys will push me out of this when it is my fight."

"It's our fight."

"And yet I'm the one with blood on my hands." She held them up as if she'd been the one to do any kind of killing.

He knelt in front of her and, though he knew it would be a mistake, took both her raised hands in his. "There's no blood here."

"There might as well be," she returned, her voice breaking on the last word. She blinked back tears. "I can't sit idly by. If you take me back there, you'll push me out. All of you."

Brady would lead that charge, but Gage didn't tell her that. He held her hands in his, irritated that both were so cold. She should have drunk the tea. He should have made her.

"No, you can't sit idly by," he agreed, if irritably. "But that doesn't mean we can't go to the ranches and work through it. Let the police do their jobs here. Let your boss do his job for the park. Back home, we'll work together to figure out what this really is. Together. I promise. No one will push you out."

She stared at him, eyebrows drawn together, frown digging lines around her mouth. Her eyes were suspicious, but she sat there and let him hold her hands. She sat there and stared at him. Thinking.

While she was *thinking*, he was *feeling* quite a bit too much.

She tugged her hands out of his grasp and stood abruptly. She stalked away from him, though it ended up being only a few steps because the cabin was so small. She whirled and pointed at him. "You promise?"

"I promise," he replied solemnly.

Because Gage Wyatt would break rules and didn't mind lying when it suited, but he wouldn't break a promise to Felicity. Not even if it killed him.

Chapter Three

Felicity sat in the passenger seat of Gage's truck, brooding over the lack of her own vehicle. The lack of her job for at least a week. The lack of her little cabin that wasn't her home exactly. It wasn't *hers* to own— it was the park's.

But neither were the ranches hers, though they made up the tapestry of her childhood and adolescence. The Wyatt boys and the foster girls of Duke and Eva Knight had run wild over both ranches. They were a piece of her, yes, but she didn't own them.

She'd gotten into the wrong business if she was worried about owning things, though. Apparently, the wrong business if she didn't want to find dead bodies.

She closed her eyes, but that only made said bodies pop up in her head, so she opened them and leaned her forehead against the window. She watched the scenery pass, from the stark browns, tans and whites of the Badlands to the verdant green and rolling hills with only the occasional ridge of rock formations that would lead them to the ranches they'd grown up on.

"Brady said for us to meet at my grandma's."

Felicity sighed. "I don't want a fuss." She didn't want all the attention or the attempts at soothing. Right now she wanted to be alone.

Except then her company would be the images of the dead bodies she'd found, and that didn't exactly appeal, either.

"Maybe it'd be a good time to tell them about our Ace connection theory," Gage offered as if he was trying to make her feel better. Which was odd coming from Gage, who was known more for making a joke out of serious things. Still, if she really thought about it, he often did that in a way that made people feel better, even if only momentarily.

"So it's *our* theory now?"

Gage lifted a negligent shoulder. "We can call it yours, but I agree with it."

"Will they?"

"Not sure. Don't see why they wouldn't. It makes sense. We'll look into it one way or another."

"*We* or you guys?"

He spared her a look as he pulled through the gate to the Reaves Ranch. Pauline Reaves had run this ranch since she'd been younger than Felicity, and though she'd married, she'd kept the ranch in her name and never let anyone believe her husband ran things.

As the story went, her late husband had been in love with her enough not to care. Felicity had never met the Wyatt boys' grandfather, who had died before Felicity had come to live with the Knights.

Felicity loved Grandma Pauline like her own. Not such a strange thing for a girl who'd grown up with the care and love of foster parents to love nonfamily like family. Pauline had always represented a strong, independent feminine ideal to Felicity. One she'd thought she'd never live up to.

But the older she got, the more Felicity felt that if she worked hard enough at it, she could be as strong and determined as Grandma Pauline. She could forge her own path.

Thoughts of Pauline's strength disappeared as the line of cars in front of Pauline's old ranch house came into view. Despite its sprawling size, piecemeal additions and modernizations over the years, and the fact only two people lived full-time in it, the house was well cared for. The boys always made sure repairs were done quickly, and Grandma kept it spick-and-span.

Still, it showed its age and wear. There was something comforting in that—or there would be if there wasn't this line of cars in front of it.

"*Everyone's* here."

"I mean, not…everyone," Gage said, trying for what she assumed was a cheerful tone.

He'd failed. Miserably. Everyone or almost everyone's vehicle being here meant something…something big at that. It was more than her stumbling across a dead body.

Felicity frowned as Gage parked in line. Based on the vehicles she recognized, Tucker and Brady were here, as was Duke and potentially Rachel and Sarah if they'd driven over with him. Dev and Grandma Pauline lived on the property, but it was Cody's truck that really bothered her. Why would he come all the way out from Bonesteel? The only vehicle missing was one belonging to Jamison and Liza. Hopefully they were at home in Bonesteel, safe and sound, taking care of Gigi, Liza's young half sister. "What is all this? Why is everyone here?"

"I don't know," he replied, sounding confused enough that she believed him. He got out of the truck and she followed. Dev's ranch dogs pranced at their feet, whimpering excitedly as they'd been trained not to bark at Wyatts or Knights.

Felicity wanted to dawdle or trudge, spend some time playing with the dogs, or maybe make a run for it to the Knight Ranch, where she knew she still had a bed waiting for her.

But that was cowardly, and it wouldn't change whatever this was. It would only avoid it for a while.

She followed Gage's brisk pace to the back door, which led to a mudroom. The dogs wouldn't follow inside at this entrance since you had to go through the kitchen to get to the rest of the house—and Grandma Pauline did *not* allow dogs in her kitchen.

Felicity stepped into the kitchen behind Gage. A very full room.

Duke and Rachel were there, sitting at the table. When Felicity had been younger, she'd been jealous of Rachel. She was Duke and Eva's only biological child, and she looked like she belonged in the Knight family. Even though with the fosters they'd been a conglomeration of black, Lakota and white—no one looking too much like anyone else—Felicity had always felt the odd man out with her particularly pale skin and bright red hair.

But she was older now, and today she was glad to see the people who were her family.

It was a little harder to be grateful for the presence of the Wyatt brothers. All of them being here in this moment only meant trouble. They brought it with them, and though they fought it as much as they could, it was always there.

Tucker stood next to Cody *and* Jamison—so they must have driven together from Bonesteel. Dev and Brady sat at the table while Grandma Pauline bustled around the kitchen.

They all looked at Felicity with smiles that were in turn sad, sympathetic or pitying. Felicity's chest got tight and panic beat through her, its own insistent drum of a heartbeat. "What's going on?"

Grandma Pauline all but pushed her into a chair and set a plate with a brownie on it in front of her. Duke took her hand and patted it.

All the eyes in the room except Gage's turned to Tucker.

His smile was the most pitying and apologetic of all. "When Brady told me what happened I asked a buddy over in Pennington County to let me know if they found anything out."

Felicity had to pause before she spoke. Getting upset often made her stutter return, but if she kept herself from rushing, she could handle it. "And they did?"

"The victim's name is Melody Harrison."

Everyone was quiet. So quiet and this was usually a noisy group.

"It's a common enough last name," Felicity forced herself to say slowly and calmly. "It might be a coincidence." She didn't know anyone named Melody, even if they shared a last name. Of course she'd been taken away from her abusive father at four. She hardly knew her biological family.

"It is common. Unfortunately, the next of kin who identified her..." If it was possible, the pitying expression grew worse. "He was her father. Michael Harrison."

"M-my father. B-but that's common, too, and—"

Tucker nodded grimly. "I confirmed it, Felicity. Your father. Melody was twenty-two, so she was born after you were placed with the Knights."

"Y-you're s-saying that..." She winced at how badly the stutter sounded in the quiet room. She made sure to take breaths between each word as she spoke. "The dead body I found is my sister."

"At least by half. Which means..." Tucker scraped a hand over his jaw.

She didn't let him say it. She might have before last year. Let him say it. Let the Wyatt boys take care of it. But no one could really take care of what was going on in her head. Even when she was weary enough to wish someone else could.

"The cops will try to connect me to it even more now."

GAGE SWORE AND felt a stab of guilt when Felicity flinched as if she'd received some kind of blow.

This was ludicrous. "How? When she didn't even know the sister existed?" Gage demanded.

His brothers gave him *that* look. The *you should know better, Gage* look. Because he was a cop. He knew how to investigate a suspicious death, and Felicity tripping over her alleged half sister was certainly suspicious.

He looked at Felicity. She'd made him promise that she wouldn't get elbowed out of dealing with this herself, so he waited for her to bring it up.

Though mostly he wanted Grandma Pauline to shove her full of brownies while he took care of everything.

However, he had enough women in his life to know they didn't particularly appreciate that method. Besides, he'd promised. So… He all but bit his tongue.

He gave Felicity a go-ahead nod, and then gestured when she simply stared at him. She blew out a slow breath.

"It could be Ace," Felicity finally said. She looked down at the plate and the brownie on it, but her voice was clear and steady no matter how little eye contact she made.

"How?" Jamison returned.

She looked up and met Jamison's gaze. "I interfered. I helped Nina and Cody. I don't know *how* it's Ace, but I know why it could be. It makes sense." Her gaze shifted to Gage, looking for some kind of support or backup.

Me not Brady. Which was very much not the point. "Obviously, the timing of the first one doesn't work, but it could be a copycat type thing. It could be a way to make it look like she's involved—and I think the family connection only makes that more plausible."

His brothers mulled that over.

"Possibly a setup. To get Felicity in trouble. A punishment for interfering," Jamison said, clearly trying to work out the logistics. "I buy that. It's Ace's MO. But how would he have orchestrated it? Since the attempt on Nina's life, we've been keeping tabs on everyone Ace talks to."

Gage had thought about that on the long, silent drive over to Grandma Pauline's. "We keep tabs on everyone who visits him in jail. Not who he talks to inside. He could be paying off a guard or threatening another inmate. Problem is, until Ace is sentenced and sent to a more secure facility, he has ample ways to outwit the system *and* us."

"His lawyer keeps getting the trial pushed back," Tucker said, disgust lacing his tone. "They're going to drag it out as long as they can."

"Don't you have any informants on the inside, Detective?" Gage asked, infusing the word *detective* with only a little sarcasm.

Tucker rolled his eyes. "Not anyone I'd trust enough to tangle with Ace."

"What do we do?" Duke asked. Demanded.

"The park forced me to take a week's leave of absence, and then they'll *reevaluate*," Felicity said miserably.

"So, you'll be home." Duke didn't have to say *where you belong* for it to be heard echoing in the silence.

Felicity smiled at Duke, but surely everyone saw how sad that smile was.

"There's not much we can do right now," Jamison said, always the de facto leader, no matter the situation. "Tucker will keep his ear to the ground when it comes to the investigation. Cody and I can look into getting some more information about who Ace talks to in the jail."

"What about…" Gage hesitated at the word *father*, considering he barely liked to call his own one. "Michael Harrison. Where did this guy come from?"

"He was the victim's father."

Gage shook his head. "That's an awful big coincidence. There was a reason Felicity was removed from his care. Was this girl?"

"Okay, point taken. We'll look into both of them."

"And what will I do?" Felicity asked, and though Gage thought she tried to turn it into a demand like Duke had done, it didn't quite hit the mark.

"Come home and rest, girl," Duke instructed.

Gage opened his mouth to come to her defense because he'd *promised*, but she shook her head.

She smiled at her foster father. "That's a good idea, Duke."

They both stood up from the table, and since she hadn't taken even a single bite of the brownie Grandma had put in front of her, Grandma immediately shoved a plastic container full of brownies into her hands.

Felicity smiled and gave Grandma a one-armed hug. "Thank you, Grandma Pauline."

"You eat, you hear me?"

"Yes, ma'am." Felicity glanced back at Gage. "Keep me up-to-date?"

He ignored the fact he got a little something out of her asking *him* and not Brady. He was very good at ignoring things he didn't particularly care for.

He gave her a nod, and Duke, Rachel and Felicity left Grandma's kitchen. Leaving Gage with his brothers and Grandma.

Dev stood first. "I've got work."

"I'll help," Gage offered. "I was supposed to anyway." He paused and looked at Jamison, Cody and Tucker. They had the best ways to get information. Gage had a few buddies over at Pennington, but Tucker knew the detectives. Jamison and Cody had been integral in getting Ace arrested in the first place, so they had a lot of ways to find information on the Ace side of things.

Gage rode the road. He had a bit too much of a mouth on him to receive the promotions Tucker and Brady seemed to rack up without even trying.

It didn't bother him. He preferred the in-the-trenches view from the bottom, but right now the lack of resources to get information made him superfluous.

So why not sweat away some frustration on ranch work? He'd spend the night, check in on Felicity tomorrow morning, then head back to his apartment to pick up his take-home car for his evening shift.

If that itch between his shoulder blades stayed there all through the afternoon and night, well, he'd deal.

WHEN HE WOKE up the next morning and trudged down to breakfast, Brady was waiting at the breakfast table. Gage rubbed bleary eyes and knew the news was bad without even a word passing between them.

"They searched Felicity's cabin," Brady said without preamble.

"And?"

"They found evidence of clothing being burned in the fire grate outside the cabin. They've collected some hair they found—clearly not Felicity's."

"Doesn't mean it's that woman's hair. That doesn't mean anything. Good Lord, she's not a suspect."

"They've sent the hair and what was left of the burnt clothes in for DNA testing," Brady said, his calm poking at Gage's agitation.

Brady sighed and shook his head, showing his first sign of emotion. "I've got a bad feeling about this."

"So do I." It smelled of a setup. But not enough of one to tip off cops who didn't know Felicity. Or Ace, for that matter.

"We've got to get her a lawyer," Brady said. With a straight face and everything.

"A lawyer? Are you insane? We have to get her out of here."

Brady's expression went carefully blank. "You can't run from the police, Gage. You *are* the police."

"Yeah, and I know this is garbage. *You* know it. Felicity wouldn't hurt a fly, and I'm not going to let her be arrested and God knows what else. Can you imagine her stuck in a cell somewhere? It's not happening."

Brady didn't move even as Gage paced the room. Cody often called them two sides of the same coin. The way they reacted, or acted in general, was often in big sweeping opposites, but when it came to it—twin junk or just the way life worked—they were the same deep down.

They might not *react* the same, but they understood.

"Where would you go?" Brady asked, without Gage even having to say he'd be the one to hide her.

"I don't know yet, but I'll figure it out."

He had to.

Chapter Four

Felicity woke up in her childhood bed. There was a deep, soothing relief in that familiarity, that cocoon of safety...for about five seconds before the anxiety started to creep in.

Luckily, there was plenty to do to keep a mind occupied when you woke up on a ranch. Though Duke and Sarah ran the cattle operation with their seasonal workers, Felicity knew a chore or two could always be picked up.

It wouldn't keep her mind from running in circles, but it might help exhaust her enough she could manage a decent night's sleep tonight instead of tossing and turning as she'd done last night.

She rolled out of bed and looked around the empty room. She'd once shared it with Sarah, but when Liza, Nina and Cecilia had all moved out, each of the remaining girls had gotten their own room instead of sharing with one other sister.

Felicity had learned how to be alone, but she did it best and most comfortably when she could be outdoors. When she could listen to birdsong and watch the stars move across the sky. When the fresh air and unique landscape made her feel *awe* at her place in the world.

Indoors, alone was just alone. Too quiet and too claustrophobic.

The thought had her walking into the hallway, determined to find someone to eat breakfast with and then find chores.

She ran into Rachel in the hallway and raised an eyebrow at her notoriously bad-at-mornings sister. "Aren't you up early."

"That class I'm teaching at the rez this summer started last week." Rachel yawned. "It might kill me."

"I thought you were going to stay with Cecilia while you did that." As a tribal police officer, Cecilia lived on the rez. Though she wasn't Duke's biological daughter, she was Eva's niece. Neither Cecilia nor Rachel would have ever said it aloud, but they had more of a connection with each other than with her, Sarah, Liza and Nina. Blood mattered, even in a foster family.

"I've been spending weeknights with Cee, and weekends here. But Daddy was grumbling last night so I stayed an extra night. I'm staying there the rest of the week after class today." Rachel yawned again, then her eyes brightened. "Hey, drive me over instead of Sarah? You can spend a few nights with us at Cecilia's, take your mind off everything. We'll have a sleepover. Sarah won't stay because of the ranch, and Liza and Nina have their girls to worry about, but the three of us could have fun."

"I don't—"

"I won't take no for an answer."

Felicity smiled. It wasn't such a bad idea. She could clear her head, enjoy her sisters. Maybe Rachel and Cecilia had a deeper connection, but Felicity only seemed to feel that when she was alone and overthinking things. When they were all together, they were sisters.

Maybe all those thoughts about deeper connections were more her own issues than the truth.

"Well, then I guess… Damn, I don't have a car."

"We'll take Duke's. He can use Sarah's truck for the weekend. You drop me off at the school, then you can do whatever. I'm sure the park will let you go back to work next week once the police have figured this out."

Felicity smiled, though she was not at all sure. Nothing about what was going on felt like last time. Last time had been a shock. It had been scary and a little traumatic, but she'd been able to convince herself it was a one-time thing. She'd just had the bad luck to be the one to find him. Bad luck was life.

Twice in two years felt a lot less like random bad luck.

"Come on," Rachel said, slipping her arm around Felicity's taller shoulders. "I'll make you breakfast. Pancakes."

"You don't have to go to all that trouble."

Rachel shrugged. "Daddy and Sarah will sing my praises. Neither of them are very good at taking care of themselves."

"What do they do when you're not here?"

"I'm hoping one of them learns through sheer necessity. I guess we'll see."

They headed downstairs together. Though Rachel

was legally blind, she knew the house so well she didn't need her support cane when walking around inside and most of the grounds outside, as well.

Duke and Sarah were likely already out doing chores, but they'd be back in a half hour or so to eat and get more coffee. Felicity set out to help Rachel make pancakes and they chatted about Rachel's art class.

It felt good and normal, and Felicity almost forgot all her worries. Everything would be fine. She had a great family. Maybe the real issue wasn't so much what had happened, but how she'd allowed herself to feel solitary and singular when she had so many people who cared about her.

Since she hadn't done anything wrong, she just had to wait out the investigation. Maybe the time off would even be good for her. She'd been so focused on having her dream job that she'd neglected her family.

She'd spend time with her sisters, with Duke, do some work around the ranch, and when she was cleared to go back to work, she'd focus more on balance.

As she turned to put the bowl of strawberries she'd just cut up on the table, she saw a truck cresting the hill to the Knight house. Not one of Duke's trucks.

"Who is it?" Rachel asked.

"Gage." Why he was suddenly the one in charge of this whole thing, she didn't know. She'd called Brady originally because she'd wanted someone to take care of it, but Brady wouldn't have just taken care of it—he would have taken over.

She'd thought she'd wanted that in the moment, but she realized as Gage's truck pulled to a stop in front of the house, she was glad Gage had included her. He'd encouraged her to speak. He believed her theories. It felt more like she was on even ground with him.

"It's early," Rachel commented. "But that doesn't mean—"

"It means he has bad news. If it's bad news, it's about the dead woman." *My sister.* Felicity really couldn't wrap her head around that part yet, so she kept pushing it away. Kept pushing the involvement of her father out of her mind. Over and over again.

Despite knowing it was coming, the knock on the door made Felicity jump.

"We could pretend we're not here," Rachel offered.

"It would only delay the inevitable. Besides, he knows we're here." Felicity steadied herself on a deep breath before opening the door.

Gage looked disheveled, which wasn't that out of character for him, but considering the circumstances it felt foreboding. His grave expression didn't help. Gage was almost never grave. He was the one who cracked a joke to break the tension or told a bizarre story to take everyone's mind off things.

Brady was the grave twin, the one who took everything seriously and was weighed down by it. She'd always admired Brady's willingness to accept responsibility.

But wasn't trying to lift the weight of a room its own kind of responsibility?

"Pack a bag," Gage said, his voice rough. "You've got five minutes before we need to be on the road."

Those harsh words, with no preamble, had Felicity frowning at him. "What are you even talking about?"

"We have to go. Now. Unless you want to spend the night, or a few nights, in jail."

GAGE SHOULDN'T HAVE put it so bluntly, but time was of the essence. He hadn't even had his coffee, which might have accounted for some of the bluntness.

"Go pack your things, Felicity," Rachel said when Felicity stood motionless.

Felicity left the kitchen at Rachel's words, and Rachel turned back to whatever she'd been doing. It looked like making pancakes.

Gage didn't know what to say in the face of a nice domestic morning Felicity should have been able to share and enjoy with her sister. This was really more of a *do* situation, and the fewer people who knew what they were doing, the better.

When Rachel turned back around, she held two travel mugs he was pretty sure were filled with coffee. *Thank God.*

She held out both to him. He stepped toward her and took them. She angled her head up, looking at him thoughtfully even though he knew she couldn't see him clearly.

The scars that had caused her loss of sight were such a part of the face he knew so well, he only noticed them now because things were bad. It made him think about all those years ago when a freak mountain lion attack had taken Rachel's sight.

Grandma had started teaching them all to shoot the

next day—Wyatt brothers and Knight girls side by side, armed with various guns and starting at ten paces away from a row of tin cans balanced on a fence.

When bad things happened, you did what you could to learn how to protect yourself from the next one. That was the lesson of his life. That was why he'd become a police officer. He knew what awful, horrible things could happen—from animal attacks to cold-blooded murder—and he'd wanted to be one of the ones who set things to right.

Sometimes he had. Sometimes he hadn't. Life wasn't perfect, and being a cop didn't mean he could fix everything, even if he wanted to.

But he could fix this for Felicity. First, he had to get her out of harm's way. Then the Wyatts would work to make sure this got cleared up. But he simply couldn't stand the thought of her in a holding cell. Not Felicity.

"You'll take good care of her," Rachel finally said.

It wasn't a question, so he didn't answer it.

Felicity returned with a backpack. She'd changed into jeans and a T-shirt and was wearing her hiking boots, which was a good thing. They'd be doing some considerable hiking. "You'll need a coat. Light one, but a coat nonetheless."

"Where are we going?"

"We'll talk about it in the truck."

She blew out an irritated breath as she walked away and then returned with a windbreaker. "Good?"

He nodded.

Felicity turned to Rachel. "Duke is going to—"

"I'll handle Daddy. You be safe."

They hugged briefly, then Felicity turned to him, grasping the straps of her backpack, a grim determination on her face. "All right. Let's go."

He led her out to his truck. He'd fixed Dev's camper shell onto his truck bed and stuffed it full of a variety of things. Hunting gear, fishing gear, ranch supplies. Hidden under all of that were two backpacks set up for backcountry camping. Brady was under strict orders to pick up the truck at the drop-off point and park it at the local airport. Make it look like he was really taking the vacation he'd lied to the sheriff about.

They reached the truck and got in. Felicity hadn't asked any questions—not that he would have answered them until they were in the truck and on their way.

She hefted her backpack into the back and folded her hands on her lap. She looked straight ahead as he started the engine.

Gage began to drive, knowing he should explain things. Instead, he took a few sips of coffee to clear his morning-fogged brain and waited for Felicity to demand answers.

"Where are you taking me?" she finally asked, which wasn't the question he thought she'd lead with.

"I figure you know some pretty isolated areas in the park we could hike to and camp without anyone finding us."

"If you backcountry camp you have to get a permit," she said primly.

He wished he could be more amused by it, but in the moment he could only be a little harsh. "Felicity.

You don't honestly think I'm going to waste my time with a permit."

"It's about safety and the park's environmental integrity. We have to know how many people—"

"Well, safety and the damn environment are going to have to take a back seat." He spared her a look, hoping it got across how dire this situation was.

"I'm a suspect," she said flatly. "We already knew that was a possibility."

God, he wished that was all it was. He rubbed a hand over the scruff on his jaw. He hadn't had a chance to shave this morning, and it didn't look like he'd be shaving any time soon.

"It's worse than that."

She swallowed. Her words were careful as she spoke, and he knew she was trying to keep her stutter under control. "How so?"

"The investigators searched your cabin."

"I d-don't have anything to hide. What does that matter?"

"They found some things anyway."

"What? How?" Felicity demanded, outrage making her cheeks turn pink. He liked it much better than the stutter, which sounded more like fear than fight.

"Someone is setting you up as a murderer." He shifted his gaze to the road. "Still want to get that permit?"

Chapter Five

Felicity didn't speak for a while after that. She let Gage drive her back to the Badlands, just as he'd driven her home from them yesterday.

Today he took the long, winding backroad to the southern portion of the park. It was far less trafficked and technically on reservation land. There would be no actual way to get into the park the way Gage was driving without doing some serious off-roading.

She looked at the grim line of his mouth and knew that was exactly his plan.

Because someone had planted evidence that she was a murderer.

A *murderer.*

The more that word spun around in her head, the more she didn't understand it. "There has to be some kind of mistake."

"What those cops found? It was no mistake. It had to have been planted, Felicity. And if it was planted, someone is purposefully trying to frame you for murder."

"It also means that poor woman was murdered."

"Felicity."

She hated the pity in his tone. *Poor, silly Felicity.* "It is still possible she just fell. It is still possible…" Yes, she was silly, because there was a part of her hoping for tragic accident over premeditated evil.

"You're the one who told me the boot in the trail was the same as the last time. Surely you knew it wasn't an accident."

"Don't you ever entertain a hope no matter how unreasonable it might be? Don't you ever think, well, *maybe* it's not as awful and dire as it looks?"

"No," he said flatly.

She didn't have to ask him why. In the silence she could hear Ace's name as if Gage had uttered it himself.

Gage had spent his formative years in the Sons of the Badlands against his will. He'd been eleven when Jamison had saved him and Brady from the gang, gotten them to Grandma Pauline. So by the time he had a real home, with an adult who truly loved him and would care for him, Gage had likely already seen too much to believe in hope.

She'd been young enough that memories of her father's beatings were vague. Sometimes she wasn't sure if they were actual memories or nightmares she'd had.

But she'd definitely been in a cast when she'd come to live with the Knights at the age of four. So, it was all true enough.

No matter her past, she could always hope for the best outcome. That's what the Knights and their love and security had given her.

"If it's Ace setting me up, I don't understand why. I don't understand."

"You said it yourself. You interfered. You helped Nina and Cody outwit his plans. That puts a big red *X* on your back, and there was already one there for being a Knight."

"But I'm not a Knight, by name or blood."

"By love you are. Which makes you a friend to the Wyatts. One who fought for us. That's all it takes to make you Ace's target."

She knew all that rationally. Though she'd assumed Ace had targeted Liza and Nina because they'd had relationships with his sons, Liza and Nina had also defied Ace's plans.

And now she'd joined their ranks.

"As for the how… I don't know how Ace does anything, let alone get hundreds of men to follow his particular brand of narcissism and contradictory insanity for years and years on end. But here we are, and you're unlucky enough to have connections to us. Maybe Ace never paid much mind to the Knights before this, but he's certainly making a case for it now."

Gage brought his truck to a stop in the middle of nowhere. Actual nowhere.

"Why are you stopping?"

"We're going to hike the rest of the way."

"And just leave your car here?"

"It'll be taken care of."

"But what if we need to get out? What if there's bad weather? Did you even pack a weather radio? Enough water? Floods, tornadoes, lightning. Rattlesnakes. You know bison are dangerous, right? And prairie dogs carry the plague."

He gave her a sardonic look and slid out of the truck without responding.

She scurried after him. There were two parts of her brain fighting it out. The one that understood he was doing what he could to keep her out of harm's way, and the part that had taken an oath to treat the park and its denizens with respect and integrity.

"Backcountry camping is serious business," she said to him in her firmest park ranger voice as he opened the camper shell on the back of the truck.

"I've been camping before," Gage replied, moving things around and barely paying any attention to her.

"Backcountry camping?"

"Yes."

"In the Badlands?"

He hefted out a sigh, stopped what he was doing and turned to her. He folded his arms over his chest, which was a distraction for a moment or two. The cuff of his T-shirt ended right at a bulge of muscle, made more impressive by the crossed-arm pose. Something wild and alarming fluttered low in her stomach.

Which wasn't important when he was talking about hiking without a permit and without taking the appropriate safety precautions.

"Sweetheart, my father left me in the Badlands for seven nights when I was seven years old. I can handle this. So can you." Then he went back to his rummaging, pulling out one backpack and then another. They were bigger backpacks than the one she'd brought—these were clearly designed for backcountry camping.

"Put anything you brought that you'll need in the green one," he said, as if he hadn't just confided something truly awful about his childhood.

Since Felicity didn't know what to say, she did as she was told. She pulled out the things she'd need: a dry set of clothes and a sweatshirt, her knife, hat, water bottle and water treatment supplies.

They were silent as she added her things to the backpack Gage had given her. He shouldered his pack, then helped her with hers, working with her to adjust the straps so it hit her where it should.

"You ready?"

She nodded, though it was a lie. She didn't think she'd ever be ready for being framed for murder. For hiking, illegally and ill prepared, through the Badlands with Gage Wyatt.

But here she was, and she'd have to face up to it. Ready or not.

GAGE THOUGHT HE'D managed to escape the uncomfortable piece of his childhood he hadn't meant to share with her. He didn't talk to anyone about his father's rituals. The initiations, the tests. Not even Brady, because though they'd had to go through them at the same times, what with being born on the same day and all, Ace had always kept them separate.

None of his brothers had ever truly discussed it. They mentioned it and laid out the bare facts when need be. But there was no looking into what it had felt like to jump through Ace's hoops.

Gage had no interest in ever going *there*.

"Why did he do it?" Felicity asked, as though she could read his thoughts.

Gage shrugged. If he never discussed it with people who'd understand, he sure wasn't going to discuss it with Felicity. But as they hiked, using a topography map and GPS tracker and his own internal sense of the land, silence ate away at his resolve to forget he'd ever brought it up.

"He called it our initiation," Gage grumbled, stopping their progress to determine if they should head east or go ahead and climb the column of rock in front of them.

"Initiation to what?"

"To the Sons." *To the Wyatt dynasty.* Gage pointed at the map, his father's voice echoing in his ears. He had to point at the map so he didn't give in to the urge to cover his ears with his hands and block out Ace's insidious voice. "What do you think? Around or over?"

Felicity peered over his shoulder. She'd fixed a baseball hat on her head and pulled her hair through the hole in the back. She'd tied her windbreaker around her waist. Underneath she wore a dark red T-shirt. She'd always been a shade too skinny, but working at the park had packed some muscle on her.

She looked more capable park ranger than inconsequential waif. It was a good look for her, one he had no business noticing at all, let alone here and now.

"Looks like around will be better," she said, reaching over his shoulder and tapping her finger on the paper. "Best place to camp is going to be over in this quadrant."

He took her advice, ignoring the flowery scent of her shampoo or deodorant or something that shouldn't be distracting but was.

They started around the column of rock. The sun was high in the sky, beating down on them. It would have been a good time to stop for water, but it seemed like a better idea to find a good spot to camp.

As far away from this conversation as possible.

"Did you want to be in the Sons?"

"Of course not," Gage snapped at the unexpected question that felt more like a dagger than a curiosity.

"I mean, when you were little. When you didn't know any better."

"I always knew better." You didn't spend most of your childhood watching your father threaten your mother's life—knowing she got pregnant over and over to keep him from going through with it—then watch her lose everything when her body simply couldn't carry another child into this world.

And you couldn't believe it was the right way of the world when you had an older brother like Jamison, who had spent his first five years with Grandma Pauline, telling you the world could be good and right.

"I'm sorry," Felicity said after a while, her voice almost swallowed by the wind. Unfortunately, not enough for him to miss it. He didn't want her apologies, or this black feeling inside of him that threatened to take his focus off where it needed to be.

He ignored her sorry and these old memories, and focused on one step in front of the other. It wasn't the first time in his life he'd counted his steps, watched his feet slap down on scrub brush. He'd thought those days were over.

But was anything ever really over? Ace could die and there would still be the mark he'd left on hundreds—if not thousands—of people.

And first on that list were six boys with the Wyatt name who had to live with what they'd come from.

"Do you know anything more about… It's just I never knew my mother. When they placed me with the Knights they said she was dead. I don't know how. I thought I didn't want to know. No. I *don't* want to know what happened to her or why. But this connects to my father. This half sister I didn't know I had and who's now dead. Who was her mother? Did my father beat her like he beat me?"

"Jamison's working on it," Gage said, trying to infuse his words with gentleness. What terrible questions to have to ask yourself.

"It should be me. I should go up to my father and ask him those things."

"Well, maybe you can at some point."

"Some point when I'm not going to get arrested, you mean?" she demanded irritably.

"Yeah, that's what I mean."

She sighed heavily next to him. "I don't ever want to talk to him."

Gage gave her a sideways glance. She wasn't just

certain, she was *vehement*. Her jaw was set, her gaze was flat and those words were final.

"Then let Jamison do the research on the woman and your father."

She wrinkled her nose, looking at her feet as they walked. "Isn't that cowardly?"

"There's nothing cowardly about your family helping you out, Felicity. Where would Jamison or Cody be if they hadn't let each other help? Where would Cody and Nina be if you hadn't helped them?"

Felicity frowned, but she nodded. "Water," she said, stopping their hike and shrugging off her pack. Gage did the same. They took a few sips from their water bottles and passed a bag of beef jerky back and forth. When they were done, Felicity dutifully sealed the empty bag in a plastic zipper bag and stored it in her pack. Ever the park ranger.

"Ready?"

She nodded, and they started hiking again, in silence for a very long time. When Felicity spoke again, he could tell it was a question she'd been turning over in her mind.

"How do we prove I didn't do it if we're all the way out here?"

Gage didn't know exactly how to respond. He'd promised Felicity the Wyatts wouldn't take over and leave her in the dark, but the nice thing about leaving people in the dark was they couldn't take actions that might undermine what you were doing until it was too late.

Still, a promise was a promise.

"This is just step one."

"Step one?"

"When they come to arrest you, the story will be you went backcountry camping to get your head on straight. By the time they send a team out to find you— if they even do, they might wait—you'll be gone."

"Gone where?"

"That's step two. Let's focus on getting through step one."

"Gone *where*, Gage?"

He sighed. There was no way getting around it. "Back to the scene of the crime."

Chapter Six

It was a very strange thing to set up camp with Gage. As a ranger Felicity had done this with all sorts of people—friends, coworkers, strangers.

But never a Wyatt.

Which shouldn't be different or feel weird. The Wyatt brothers were her friends. She'd shared meals and *life* with them.

Trying to convince herself this was all normal came to a screeching halt when they had everything unpacked. "Wait. There's only one tent."

She looked at Gage, a vague panic beginning to beat in the center of her chest. He merely raised an eyebrow, the sunset haloing him in a fiery red that made the panic drum harder.

"Safest if we're in the same tent," he said after a while.

She wasn't sure how to describe the sound that escaped her—something strangled and squeaky all at the same time.

"Problem?"

"No. No. *No.* Of course there's no *problem.*" There

was a catastrophic, cataclysmic event happening inside of her, but no *problem*.

"Afraid I'm going to try something?"

She tried a laugh, which came out more like a bird screech. "I like Brady," she blurted, as if that had anything to do with *anything*.

"I'm very well aware."

"And you like…" She thought of the women she'd seen Gage with. Rare. He never brought girlfriends home.

Still, every once in a while for a birthday or something, the Wyatt boys and Knight girls would get together in town. Go to a bar or something. Gage's dates were always… "You like breasts."

He choked out a laugh. "Yeah. Crazy that way. Hate to break it to you, you have those."

She looked down, even though of course she *knew* she had breasts. Not ever on full display or anything, but yes, she had them. They were there. And why was *she* looking at them while her face turned what had to be as red as the sunset?

Had Gage noticed her breasts? Why did that make her feel anything other than horrified?

"If it bothers you, I can sleep outside."

"It doesn't *bother* me." She was pretty sure she'd have the same ridiculous reaction to sharing a tent with Brady. Sharing a tent was *intimate* and she didn't have an intimate relationship with…

Anyone.

But there was one tent up, and perfectly rational reasons for them both sleeping in it. It would be fine, regardless of the jangling nerves bouncing around inside of her. She'd survived those for almost her whole life, even learned to overcome them for the most part.

She was struggling today because people thought she was a murderer. Someone was trying to make it look like she was a murderer. It was messing with her brain in many different ways, not just one.

"Hungry? I can cook up some dinner," Gage said, acting as though this was normal and fine and not at all scary and weird.

"I hope you know you can't have a campfire. Backpacking stove only. We can't go breaking every park rule just because we're in trouble."

Gage didn't respond. His mouth quirked, his eyebrow raised, and he pulled a backpacking stove out of his pack.

Brady never did that arched eyebrow thing. Brady's lip never quirked in that sardonic way at her. And his eyes never went quite that shade of brown, as if there was a hidden intensity under all that…

What on earth was *wrong* with her?

She was camping with Gage to avoid being arrested for a murder she darn well didn't commit.

"Park rules are important," she insisted, though he hadn't argued. "People try to get away with all sorts of things that hurt the cultural and ecological integrity of the land and threaten the safety of the park."

"Believe it or not, I'm well versed in what people will try to get away with."

"I suppose you think your laws are more important than mine?"

He cocked his head as he set up the stove and measured out water into a pot. "Why do you assume that?"

"Because…" She trailed off because she didn't have a good answer. Gage had never given any indication he thought his job was more important than hers. Nor had any of the other significant people in her life. Certainly she'd had a few park visitors who liked to sneer at how not important she was to them, but—

"Sit. Eat. Stop…that."

She blinked at him, startled by him interrupting her thoughts. "Stop what?"

"Whatever it is you're doing standing there with your mind whirling so hard I can *hear* it."

"You cannot hear my brain."

"Near enough. If you're going to occupy yourself, might as well focus on the problem at hand, not how much more you'd rather spend a night in a tent with Brady than me."

"That isn't what…" But she couldn't explain in a way that made any sense.

She acquiesced and sat, then took the tin bowl he offered her. She *was* hungry. Tired, too. And though she knew he couldn't *hear* her brain moving, it felt like it was galloping around at rapid pace, and she wasn't sure why.

She'd sleep under the same canvas roof as Gage Wyatt. So what?

So someone wanted to frame her for murder—she had a big group of people willing to help her prove she hadn't actually done it. She had Gage to make sure she didn't spend a night in jail.

They ate in silence, watching the sun go down. It might have been peaceful, but she didn't feel any kind of peace. Just anxiety and something else. Something edgier and sharper than the sheer manic ping-ponging of anxiety.

"He doesn't get you, Felicity," Gage said quietly, staring intently at the bowl in his lap as the last whispers of light faded away. "I'm not saying that to be cruel. I just think you could find a lot better focus for your... It's not going anywhere."

It took her a minute to realize he was talking about Brady, and then another minute before full realization hit.

She couldn't find the words to argue.

"He can't ever..." Gage swore under his breath. "Brady is too noble to ever see you as anything other than Duke's foster daughter."

It should hurt. She should be outraged and embarrassed and feel horrible. Intellectually, she told herself that. But there was no crushing pain of a heart breaking. No heated moral outrage that he didn't know what he was talking about.

She was under no illusion Brady looked at her and saw the real *her*. She'd never asked herself why she liked him anyway, why she convinced herself he might someday.

It wasn't comfortable that Gage had been the one to point out having a crush on Brady didn't make much sense. Her face was on fire, and she couldn't find a way to defuse her embarrassment.

She didn't think Gage's words were cruel. In fact, she knew he was trying to be kind. Trying to show her it was never happening.

She was in the middle of the stark Badlands with his twin brother of all people telling her things she already knew.

Because she did know. She told herself she didn't. She told herself she was holding out hope for Brady to come around, but she was aware of the truth.

Brady was safe. In more ways than one. Safe because he wasn't edgy or volatile. Because he was exactly what Gage said. Too noble to ever consider one of Duke Knight's daughters in a romantic way.

She didn't want Brady in reality. She liked the idea of him. Liked pining after him. She could tell herself she had normal feelings for a guy and never actually have to deal with it. *Know* she'd never ever have to deal with him reciprocating.

The truth was Brady was never going to break his code of honor and see her as different—and she'd known that.

She'd liked him *because* she'd known that.

"Maybe I don't need him to get me," she managed to say, when what she really meant was, *Maybe I don't want anyone to know me*.

Gage shrugged. "None of my business," he muttered.

Which was more than true. Totally and utterly true.

She couldn't for the life of her understand why he'd brought it up.

GAGE DID NOT sleep well. The tent was small, and it smelled like a woman. He'd never camped with a woman before.

Never will again.

Maybe if you were all wrapped up in the woman it would be nice enough, but with a platonic friend you had some more than *companionable* feelings for it was too crowded, too all-encompassing. Who'd want to be right on top of anyone like this?

He looked at Felicity, who was fast asleep only a few feet away from him.

She was too pale—he could tell that even in the odd cast the faint light made against the blue nylon of the tent. Her freckles were more pronounced than usual, and though she slept deeply and quietly there were shadows under her eyes.

He felt a stab of guilt, a twist of worry that he'd done something rash without fully considering the consequences. He'd put her through too much just so she didn't have to spend a few nights in jail.

Jail. Whether it was a holding cell or the facility Ace was at, she'd look worse in there. She was an outdoorsy person. Better to be hiking through the rigorous Badlands backcountry than locked in a cell, that he knew for sure.

Thunder rolled in the distance, making the tent seem all that more intimate.

Felicity's eyes blinked open, and he knew he should probably look away. Try to pretend he wasn't a creeper staring at her while she slept.

But he didn't.

Worse, she stared right back. For ticking seconds that had his breath backing up in his lungs. Her green eyes were dark and reminded him of Christmas trees, of all damn things.

"It's raining," she said quietly, still holding his gaze.

"So it is."

She pushed herself up into a sitting position. Her red hair tumbled behind her, the rubber band she'd had it fastened back with yesterday falling onto the floor between them. She didn't seem to notice.

Gage couldn't help it. He reached out, picked up the band and held it out to her. She took it with one hand, patting the unruly state of her tangles with the other.

He watched a little too closely as she bundled it back behind her, fastening the band around it again. Then way too closely at the way her shirt pulled over her breasts.

He looked up at the top of the tent and blew out a breath. Rain pattered there and he focused on counting the drops, on considering how heavy the rain was and if they should hike today or stay put. Anything that wasn't this totally pointless, impossible attraction to the woman head over heels in love with his twin brother.

Yeah, it figured he was *that* messed up.

"If we go out today, we'll have to be very careful," Felicity said primly.

He didn't dare look at her, because something about that park-ranger-lecturing voice really did something to him.

He was *seriously* messed up in the head.

"You know, the Badlands are made up of bentonite

clay and volcanic ash. Which means, when it rains the rocks become very slip—" She stopped herself, frowning at him. "What are you grinning at?"

He shook his head, trying to wipe the smile off his face. "Nothing."

"You're grinning about *something*."

"You don't want to hear it from me."

"What does *that* mean?" she demanded, hands fisted on her hips, though she was kneeling.

He should keep his mouth shut. Go outside into the storm if he had to, but that would be stupid. Almost as stupid as the words that tumbled out of his mouth. "I just remember when you couldn't string two sentences together—especially around a Wyatt—without turning bright red and running to hide in your room. It's nice you found your passion. Even if it's bentite clay."

"Bentonite."

"Right. Sure." He couldn't help laughing. "You're doing all right, Felicity. That's all I'm saying."

"Why wouldn't I want to hear that from you?"

"Anyone else notice?"

She squared her shoulders as if gearing up for a fight. "I don't need anyone to notice."

"But I did notice, is all I'm saying. And I like it." Which was better than everything he wanted to say, like *and I'd like my hands all over you*.

Their gazes met and held. She opened her mouth as if she was going to say something to that, but no sound emerged.

He should say something. A joke. God, he should tell a joke, but it was as if every coping mechanism he'd built to defuse a tense situation had evaporated simply because he'd spent the night under the same fabric roof as her.

She cleared her throat and looked away. "What's the plan? It isn't safe to stay here with a storm. You do have a weather radio, don't you?"

"I wouldn't think it'd be safe to go hiking through a storm, either," he said, opening his pack and rummaging around until he found the radio. He tossed it to her.

She fiddled with it and he unzipped the door. They had a rain flap, and he could feel the wind blowing in the opposite direction. He could use some fresh air and a glimpse at how heavy the storm was looking.

He heard the static of the weather radio, then the low, monotonous tones of someone going on about warnings and watches.

"Gage."

"What?" He reached for his gun, sure that the gravity and fear in her voice meant there was someone coming, a physical, human threat. But as he turned to her, she was pointing at the sky.

And a very distinct funnel cloud.

Chapter Seven

For precious seconds, every training Felicity had ever received on the subject of what to do in case of bad weather simply fell out of her head. Her mind was blank as she watched the distinct form of a funnel cloud whirl on the horizon.

It was far away now, but it wouldn't stay that way.

Fear and dread skittered up her spine. She knew fear and dread—had been born into it. It was acknowledging the feelings when reality sank in—whether it was the violent look in her father's eye or a funnel cloud, first was fear.

Then, she'd learned to act.

"We need to break down the tent and get to lower ground, but not too low. More rain could come in right after it and we don't want to be caught in any flash flooding," she shouted above the sound of the wind and rain.

"You load up both packs and I'll take care of the tent," Gage said. It felt less like an order and more like two people working together to survive.

Lightning flashed, something sizzled far too close,

and thunder boomed immediately after—the hard crack echoing in her ears.

Her hands shook as she shoved the weather radio back into Gage's pack and hurried to roll the sleeping bags into their sacks. He had the tent down in record time, which left her open to the elements. She pulled up the hood of her windbreaker.

Fat drops fell from the sky on their packs and their bodies. Felicity looked at the funnel cloud. It was still there. Closer.

"Rain is a good sign," she said, knowing it was more hope than reality. "It means the funnel itself is still a long way off."

"Is it?" Gage returned, shoving the packed tent into his pack. "None of this feels like too good a sign." He settled a cowboy hat on his head and looked around. "Where to, Ranger?"

She'd looked at the topographic map when they'd camped last night and oriented herself to the area. She'd listened to the weather radio and tried to get an idea of the trajectory of the storm. "Follow me."

Though they hiked in silence, the storm raged around them. Thunder booming, lightning cracking and sizzling too close. She let out a screech against her will when she *saw* lightning strike in front of her.

"Steady," Gage said, his voice low and close to her ear. "All that slippery benzonite."

"Bentonite," she ground out as her heart beat so hard against her chest it felt like a hammer trying to break through her rib cage.

The rain slowed, the noise quieted. The air got still

and the sky was tinged an unearthly green. Felicity walked, forcing herself to breathe slowly in and out as she began to shake with fear.

"Don't look back," Gage ordered.

She listened, because she knew what was coming. Especially when the still silence suddenly turned into a slow-building roar.

"We should take cover," Felicity shouted over the thundering wind. Dust swirled around them and she had to close her eyes against the debris flying into her face. "We can't keep walking."

"There isn't any cover."

"Kneel. Put your pack over your head—just like tornado drills in school."

"I—"

There was the sickening sound of a blow and a grunt. Felicity whirled around and out of the corner of her eye saw Gage go down. He stumbled, rolled and hit the ground too hard.

He was swearing when she skidded down next to him, which she'd take as a good sign. Swearing meant breathing and consciousness.

"Don't move," she ordered, still having to yell over the sound of wind and rock.

He swore some more, most of it lost to the roaring tornado around them, while he followed her instructions and didn't move.

He was bleeding from a nasty cut on his temple, but it didn't look deep enough to worry over a severe head injury.

"Can you roll onto your stomach?"

He didn't respond, but he rolled over.

"Loosen your straps," she instructed, already scooting up so she could reach his pack. "I'm going to pull your pack up to cover the back of your head."

Small rocks and dust pelted her, seemingly from all sides, though nothing like what had taken Gage down. He grunted as he got the straps off his arm, and she tugged the pack up to cover the most vulnerable part of his head.

Then she lay down next to him and situated her own pack over the back of her head and neck. She closed her eyes and focused on her breathing.

It reminded her too much of a time she'd tried to forget. The first four years of her life. They were a blur and she had always been happy to leave them that way. Eyes closed, careful breathing, and terror ripping through her while noise raged around her...

She could remember, clearly, hiding in the back of a utility closet. It had smelled like bleach, and she'd scrambled behind mops and brooms. He'd found her. The creak of the door, the spill of light that didn't quite make it to her.

And still unerringly he'd stepped forward and grabbed her by her shirt and dragged her out of the closet. For a few seconds, she was back there, struggling against her father, against the inevitable.

Then a hand closed over hers. In the here and now and roaring winds. She opened her eyes to look at Gage. Blood was trickling down his face since he was lying on the uninjured side. And he was trying to give her some comfort.

"I've survived worse," he rasped over the sound of the tornado.

"Have you?"

"Human nature is worse than Mother Nature."

Felicity shook her head as much as she could in her prone position. "You don't know enough about Mother Nature then, Gage."

She had no idea if he'd heard her, but she didn't let go of his hand, and he didn't let go of hers. As the world heaved around them, they held on to each other.

She wasn't sure how long they lay there or how much longer after that the roar faded into a light wind and pattering rain. The rumble of thunder was distant.

Eventually she felt the groundwater begin to seep into her pants and knew they had to get up. She gave Gage's hand a squeeze before letting it go, then got to her knees. She looked around.

The Badlands stretched out before them looking no different than it had before the tornado had blown through. In the distance, the sun peeked out from the clouds, its rays shining down in clear lines.

Felicity let out a long breath. They'd survived.

"Hopefully, it stayed out here," she murmured to herself. Out here in the Badlands, nature took its course and few things were irrevocably harmed. Tornadoes and extreme thunderstorms were *part* of the shape and heart of the landscape.

But Pennington County and the reservation were in the path of the tornado. People and things could be irrevocably damaged. People and things she loved, even.

But before she could worry about that, she had to worry about Gage.

She tugged the pack off him. "Can you sit up?"

He didn't answer in words. He rolled to his side and leveraged himself up, wincing and swearing. Then swearing some more when she moved to help him.

"Don't stand yet," she said, pushing him against the rock behind him. "Sit right here so I can clean you up."

"You're beautiful. Both of you."

She startled for a second, then shook her head, realizing he was attempting a joke despite the fact blood still oozed from the cut on his temple. "That's some head injury."

"I see double. But at least I'm not blind, right?"

"Not exactly the joke I'd make right now, Gage."

"That's my job. Make the joke no one else would make. Get a little laugh to diffuse the terror."

She felt both relief he was trying to make light of the situation and a bone-deep worry at how much blood was on his face, how deep the cut was under further inspection, and the fact he hadn't even tried to get to his feet.

She rummaged in her pack and retrieved the first-aid kit. She couldn't waste potable water on washing blood off his face, so she had to hope the antibacterial wipes would be enough. She crouched in front of him with some regret.

"Not to sound like a cliché, but this is going to hurt."

IT DAMN WELL DID. He hissed out a breath as she pressed the antibacterial wipe to the nasty wound on his head.

He didn't know what had hit him, a rock probably. It had been sharp and hard and taken him down in the same way. His neck and back hurt, probably from the fall.

And the fact you aren't getting any younger.

"I'm sorry," she murmured, wiping the blood off his face. The wound throbbed and stung in turns, but Felicity's fingers were on his face and that wasn't so bad.

"A pretty woman is patching me up. I'll survive."

Her worried expression transformed into a frown. "Stop saying that."

"What?"

"Beautiful and pretty. You don't need to suck up to me. I'm going to tend your wound either way."

"Don't you think you're beautiful and pretty?"

She stared at him for a good minute, her mouth hanging slightly open. "I... Oh, just shut up and let me do this."

He smiled, couldn't help it. Irritated Felicity made him feel better.

No matter her annoyance, her hands were gentle as she wiped up as much blood as she could and then applied the bandage. She touched his forehead and his cheekbones as if checking for more damage.

He watched her, woozy enough that he didn't even try to hide that his attention was on her face. On her, fully and wholly.

She finally looked him in the eye, opening her mouth to say something. But it evaporated before any sound came out. For seconds they simply stared at each other, silent and still, stuck in the moment.

He couldn't remember the last time he'd felt this. Middle school maybe. The desperate need to *do* something. Make a move, because it felt almost as if he'd cease to exist if he didn't. A profound fear of coming up short left him frozen in place.

Because he wasn't Brady, and Brady was always the better option. Gage was more of a backup.

Felicity deserved first prize, even if that particular prize didn't have a clue of the woman she'd become.

Felicity straightened, stepped back and wiped her hands on her pants. She looked around. The rain had tapered off, and though clouds mostly covered the sun, it occasionally broke out in soft rays as the clouds moved with the furious wind.

"We need help. We need cell service." She nodded with each sentence as if making her own mental list.

"Good luck on that front."

"We should consolidate to one pack. Your vision is messed up so your balance will be off. I'll carry one pack—water is most important. We're going to be slow moving, but I know where to go. We can hopefully get to cell range before nightfall."

"I can carry my own pack. My vision is fine." He blinked a few times. The doubling came and went, but he could walk just fine.

"No. It isn't smart. We have to be smart."

Gage struggled to his feet, ignoring the wave of dizziness and making sure not to reach out for balance. She was watching him too closely and he needed to prove to her he was fine so she didn't worry. So she didn't try to help.

"One pack," she muttered, crouching in front of the two packs, and pulling things out and shoving other things back into hers. "We'll mark this place on the map and come back for what we leave."

He watched her move—each gesture jerky. Each sentence sounded a little more... *Tight* was the only word he could think of. Like there was some invisible string pulling her in tighter and tighter.

Until she broke. Except Felicity wasn't going to break. He could see that as she babbled on and on about what they had to do. She would keep that rein on control through this whole thing, then be left with a hell of a breaking point when all was said and done.

He knew her well enough to realize she'd see that as a failure, especially if she broke in front of their family or whoever finally picked them up.

He wanted her to break now. She'd still be embarrassed that it was in front of him, but it wouldn't be as bad as Duke or her sisters or the whole Wyatt clan.

"Felicity. Take a breath."

"I'm breathing," she retorted, as he'd predicted. She made a move to sling the newly rearranged pack onto her shoulders, but he grabbed it and pulled it off her.

"Hey, I said I was going to—"

He dropped it on the ground to the side of them and stepped toward her. She scrabbled back, almost tripping in the process.

"What are you doing?" she screeched.

He didn't answer, because the more she worked herself up the better chance she had of actually letting it go.

Gently he folded her into his arms. "We're okay," he murmured. He rubbed a hand up and down her back, cupped the back of her head and held her there against him as she struggled a bit. He understood the manic look in her eyes, understood what she needed to do before they moved on. "We're okay."

"I know it," she squeaked, wriggling against his hold. But her breathing was ragged and it only took a few more seconds of holding her there for her to break. A sob, the slow surrendering of her forehead to his chest.

"That's it," he murmured, resting his cheek against her hair. "Let it out."

She did. As he held her there, hand in her hair, cheek on her hair. Soft and curling against his own skin. He wanted with an ache he didn't fully understand because it was so deep, so wide, so *nonsensical*.

Still, he held her while she cried, and though time wasn't in their favor he didn't rush her. He let her have her moment.

Finally, she pulled away with a sniffle, wiping at her cheeks with her palms. "I'm stronger than that," she muttered.

"Nothing weak about crying. I mean, I know that goes against Grandma Pauline's code of badass conduct, but I've helped too many people in too many dire situations to not know crying is essential sometimes."

"Eva always said so. More to Sarah than the rest of us."

"Sarah tries too hard to be tough," Gage returned, speaking of the youngest Knight foster.

"She comes by it honestly, between being Duke's second hand on the ranch and helping Dev when he needs it."

"Maybe we should lock her and Dev in a room and tell them we won't let them out till one of them shows an emotion that isn't categorized as pissed-off grumpy."

Felicity chuckled, which had been his hope. She sucked in a breath and let it out loudly. "All right. We've got a long way to hike."

"You're in charge."

She gave him a suspicious look. "Really?"

"You know where you're going and, frankly, you're better with that kind of map than I am. So, lead the way, Ranger. You'll get us where we need to be."

She blew out a breath and nodded. "All right. Follow me and be careful. One injury is enough."

She was right about that.

Chapter Eight

The hike was brutal. The rocks were slippery, and they couldn't find much grass to walk on instead. Added to that, no matter what Gage said, he was clearly not at 100 percent. He was slow and he'd stopped arguing about her being the only one carrying a backpack.

Felicity hated to admit it, but crying it out had certainly calmed her. She felt exhausted but determined. Worried but not panicked. They would get where they needed to go, even if Gage wasn't 100 percent.

Because she was.

She eyed the sun, and how quickly it was heading for the horizon. Maybe they'd have to hike at dark for a bit. Dangerous, but so was surviving a tornado blasting through the Badlands. Which they'd done with only minor injuries.

"How you holding up?" she asked. Though she wanted to look back and get an idea for herself, they were in a particular slippery canyon area. One wrong step would mean a nasty fall. So, she listened carefully to his response and any pain that might be threading through his voice.

"Fine and dandy, gorgeous," he said breezily.

She gripped the straps of her pack, trying to tamp down her irritation. "Stop that."

"But see, now that I know it irritates you I *can't* stop."

She kept her gaze on the landscape in front of her. If he was joking around he couldn't be that bad off. "This isn't a joking situation, Gage."

"Well, it's not a joke. It's me saying something true that irritates you for some reason," he returned so *reasonably*, as if it was reasonable when it wasn't at all. "Anything can be a joking situation if you're funny enough."

She knew there had to be a good response for that, but she couldn't find it. Not even a lecture about jokes.

Both their phones began to chirp, and they stopped in their tracks.

"We should probably keep hiking and get to the ranger station before dark," Felicity said. No matter how badly she wanted to check their phones, they were running out of good hiking time.

"People are worried about us, Felicity," Gage returned.

When she turned around to lecture him, he already had his phone to his ear. She eyed the sun again, then took out her own phone.

She had fifty text messages, ten missed calls and five voice mails. She winced, then began to type out a text to everyone at the ranch that she was okay. Something quick, then they could be on their way again.

But Gage swore, so vehemently that Felicity stopped midtap.

"What is it?"

He shook his head, held up a finger and returned the phone to his ear. "Jamison. You've got to be kidding me with that message," he said viciously into the receiver. He paused, his expression fury personified as he listened to whatever Jamison was saying in return. "Yes, we're fine. What's being *done*?"

He was silent for so long Felicity had to bite her tongue to keep from demanding answers immediately. He was getting them. She had to be patient.

"Stay put. Take care of your own. We'll handle us." He ended the conversation and shoved his phone into his pocket.

When he didn't immediately speak, she stopped holding back. "Gage. Tell me what is going on."

He shook his head, his jaw working for a few seconds before he finally spoke. "The tornado hit the jail."

Felicity felt as if the ground fell out from underneath her and she was descending through an endless canyon. Though she was standing on her own two feet, the sound of the long-gone tornado roared in her ears. "What?"

"It hit the jail in Pennington. Ace is unaccounted for."

"As in dead or as in…"

"Escaped. He's not the only one." Gage shoved a hand through his unruly dust-covered hair. "But he's the one we have to worry about."

"All right. We have to get back," Felicity said, doing

her best to sound calm and sure. "Back to the ranches, work out a game plan with everyone."

"If our theory about Ace being involved in framing you for murder is correct, he's coming for *you*, Felicity."

That revelation hit hard, but she wouldn't let it show. She straightened her shoulders and firmed her mouth. "If he's behind this trumped-up murder charge, hasn't he already hurt me enough? He won't be after me—he already got me. He'll be after one of you."

Gage stared at her for a long time before finally inclining his head. "Fair point."

It felt like a victory when none of this was a victory. It was only problem after increasingly threatening problem.

"Okay, we head back to the ranch," Felicity said. "Someone can pick us up at the ranger station. It's better if we're all there, working together to keep everyone safe from Ace. Especially Brianna and Gigi." Cody and Nina's daughter and Liza's half sister had already been through enough.

"If you show up at either ranch, you'll be arrested."

Felicity tried to play off the wince inside of her. "I...I can handle that. You should be with your family." She tried to smile, though she knew it faltered.

She could handle jail. She could handle it because she knew she was innocent. It was fine. Okay, *fine* was an overstatement. But it would be bearable. She could bear it. She could. Because eventually the truth would come out.

Eventually.

"I'm not letting you go to jail, Felicity. Not ever."

She blinked at his sheer vehemence. Her entire stomach seemed to flip over at the look in his eyes.

She didn't know what that was. Didn't want to know because it scared her. It…vibrated through her. Too big and too much.

"It wouldn't be so bad," she choked out.

"If they convicted you, do you understand how many years you could be stuck in there? Do you have any idea how long it would be before you could come out here?" He pointed to the land around them. "Think about it—you'll come to the same conclusion I did."

She looked around at the Badlands, at the vast gray, moody sky. At her heart, laid out in the world around them, even when it did things like throw a tornado at her. "I wouldn't survive," she murmured.

She didn't need anyone to understand her, to see her as the woman she'd become because *she* knew who and what she'd built herself into. Being a somewhat solitary person meant she didn't need people to constantly validate her choices or tell her she was doing great.

But she hadn't realized how nice it would be to have one person actually…get her. Not in some demanding way, not showing off how much. Just a simple, true understanding.

She didn't know how to fully accept that it was *Gage*, who was nothing like her. He was all confidence, with a certain brashness that *was* charming but certainly nothing she understood.

How could he look at her and see…it all?

She didn't want to know. She didn't want to think

about it, but all she could seem to do was stand here and stare at him, something big and bright and terrifying shifting in her chest.

Ace was free, and she was wanted for murder. That was her focus right now.

Or so she told herself.

FELICITY LOOKED AT him like his understanding was some kind of gift when it couldn't be. When his father was on the loose, with everyone he loved a target.

Including her.

Not that Gage was *in love* with her. Liking and appreciating someone and being attracted to someone did not add up to *love*.

Besides, loving anyone while Ace existed was a pain and fear he didn't intend to take on. He'd watched Jamison and Cody survive, barely, and maybe they were happier on this side of things, but how could that fear of Ace really ever go away?

It couldn't. It didn't. Not until the man was dead. Gage was half convinced he'd never die.

"All right," Felicity said at length. She sounded shaky at first, then her voice strengthened as she spoke. "Still, you're hurt. You need to go back and have that looked at."

"Hey, I can still see. I can still walk. Cody did a lot more with a lot worse."

"Because he had to," Felicity said with a gentleness that made his skin tight and prickly.

"Are you suggesting I leave you out here on your own?" he asked, trying to keep the sheer volume of rage out of his voice. All that rage wasn't directed at her—it was at Ace, and himself—but he was in danger of losing it anyway.

"It wouldn't be the first time I've hiked, camped and survived the Badlands on my own, Gage."

"It won't be *this* time, either," he returned. "Listen to me. There's no splitting up here. No leaving anyone on their own. That isn't how you beat Ace. Haven't Jamison and Cody proven that? We have to work together best we can. And whether you like it or not, you and me are together for this one."

She didn't respond as she chewed on her lip and mulled it over. He couldn't stand the quiet, so he kept on her.

"Jamison and Cody are going to protect Liza, Gigi, Nina and Brianna in Bonesteel. The rest of my brothers will be at the ranches with Grandma Pauline and your family. It makes sense for us to keep to our plan. We have to prove you didn't murder this woman."

He took a step toward her, told himself at the last minute not to grab her hands like he wanted to. "Just think. If we prove this—we can go home to the ranches. Ace being on the loose makes things nerve-racking. But it doesn't change our objective. It doesn't change what *we* have to do."

"I don't want to be the reason you're not working with your brothers on this."

He didn't understand the things she did to him. He'd avoided personal vulnerability all his life because, good Lord, life was too tough to be worried about weakness.

She was tough, but she was also…this: the broken little kid underneath all that tough exterior.

He understood it too well.

"We're in this together, Felicity. Now, how long will it take us to hike to your cabin?"

"Days."

He knew it was long, but he'd been hoping doable. They couldn't hike days. Especially after leaving one pack behind.

"Another park ranger would give us a ride if we get to the visitor center," she said, though she sounded uncertain.

"Are there any park rangers you trust? That you're willing to put in the path of both the police *and* Ace?"

She wilted. "No."

He didn't want one of his brothers making the trek, which had been the original plan. With Ace on the loose, they needed to stick together, protect Grandma and the Knights. Having one or even two come pick them up was risking too much.

"What about Cody's group?" Felicity asked. "Nina said there was some woman who helped them, and Brady mentioned a doctor who video chatted him through patching Cody up. Call Cody and see if they can help. Even if they can just offer a ride if we can meet them a little south of the visitor center."

"If they can't, he'll come himself."

"Not if you remind him his job is to protect Nina and Brianna."

It wasn't the worst idea. Besides, what would it hurt to ask?

"We have to keep hiking, though," Felicity insisted. "The minute we lose daylight, we're in for trouble. I had to prioritize water over sleeping bags and dry clothes in the pack. We can eat and we can drink, but we won't have any way to protect ourselves if another storm comes through."

He studied the sky. Another storm seemed more likely than not. Hopefully, they'd survived their one and only tornado, but rain and lightning could be just as dangerous in the wrong circumstances.

"All right," he finally acquiesced. Her plan was sound, and it was a compromise between what they both wanted to do. "I'll text Cody, then we'll get moving."

"You text him. I'm going to change your bandage." She dropped her pack and rummaged around in it while he texted Cody to ask for backup south of the visitor center.

She pulled off the bandage slowly, clearly trying to keep the adhesive from hurting his skin.

It was hard to focus on the throbbing pain when her chest was in his face and he had much more entertaining things to distract himself with.

"I'm worried about infection more than the cut itself," she said conversationally as she used another stinging wipe around the wound.

He bit his tongue to keep from hissing or groaning in pain, then let out a slow, steady breath as she smoothed a new bandage over the cut.

"There." She cupped his chin and tilted his head up as she examined the bandage. She gave a little nod, clearly satisfied with her work. She brushed at his scruffy jaw, presumably trying to get dirt and debris out of his whiskers, but her other hand gently traced the bandage.

He was sure she was making sure no dirt had gotten into the bandage, but it felt like a caress. Like she cared. And his libido certainly didn't seem to know the difference between *trying to stave off infection* and *trying to get in his pants.*

Irritated, he squirmed. "If you expect me to be able to walk straight, you're going to have to stop touching me like that."

She pulled her hand away so fast her whole body jerked and she stepped back, landing awkwardly on a rock. She started to fall backward, arms windmilling, so he grabbed her and yanked her toward him.

Which sent her bumping into him, sending *him* falling backward. Luckily, he knew how to land after a blow well enough. Unluckily, she was now sprawled on top of him.

She was on top of him, breathing a little heavily, her eyes wide and her cheeks pink. He thought not kissing her might kill him.

But she wants Brady.

"I'm going to get you out of this mess." He didn't know why he had to promise her that, to vow it here and out loud. He just had to get it out. Better than kissing her, he had to believe.

She stared at him, green eyes dark and steady, still

lying on top of him, soft and warm and wonderful. "I believe you," she said quietly.

And he was doomed. So he went ahead and pressed his lips to hers anyway.

Chapter Nine

Felicity had never walked through fire before, but she was pretty sure it would feel like this. Completely enveloped by sensation.

In this case not burning to a crisp, painful and fatal, but melting into someone else entirely. Maybe it *was* fatal—she wasn't sure—but she couldn't help following it. The wild sensation of freedom like standing in the middle of grass and rock with no one else around. Just her and the wind and sky and utter glory.

Except it was Gage. *Gage.* Gage Wyatt. Kissing her. Kissing *her.*

She blinked her eyes open, trying to push herself off him. He stopped kissing her, but his hand curled around her arm, keeping her in place.

"We have to… Getting dark," she croaked.

He did his raised-eyebrow thing, and all she wanted to do was run away from him, but his big hand was still curled around her upper arm, keeping her all sprawled out against him. He was very…hard and warm and… She had to get up.

"Hike. Before dark. We need to get moving."

"You kissed me back."

"I…" She didn't know what to say to that. How to process *any* part of today. "L-let me go."

He did. Immediately. She scrabbled off him and onto her feet. She was shaky and shaken, and God knew she didn't have a clue what to say.

Gage had kissed her. Voluntarily. And…seriously. Devastatingly. Like he'd been waiting half a lifetime to do it.

Oh, boy. Oh, no.

If she went home she would be arrested for a murder she didn't commit, and Gage Wyatt had kissed her.

She *knew* she hadn't killed anyone, and as much as the world wasn't always right and good, she simply had to believe someone could prove that.

What she didn't know was how to deal with this… kiss.

She'd let Asher Kinfield kiss her when she'd worked at Mammoth Cave for a summer. It had been nothing like this. It had been kind of stiff and fumbling. Off-putting.

Not like fireworks. No, bigger than fireworks. A volcanic eruption. Destructive and totally altering.

All because of Gage Wyatt.

She looked back at him as he got to his feet. She'd jerked away not so much because of his words. More because she'd lost herself in touching him and had forgotten she was supposed to be bandaging him up, not caressing his wounds. She *had* been touching him like a lover, and she didn't know what on earth had possessed her.

Gage stared at her, his face hard and unreadable. "I'm not Brady," he said sharply.

That snapped through some of her panic. She scowled at him, insulted and maybe even hurt. She couldn't name half the feelings pulsing inside of her. "I was under no illusion you were, *Gage.*"

"You sure about that?"

"Yes." She grabbed the pack and fastened it onto her back with jerky movements. She was not going to argue with him about Brady. She hadn't even *thought* of Brady until Gage had brought him up. "W-we have to m-move."

She didn't wait to see if he followed, and she refused to acknowledge her stutter. She started marching along, carefully avoiding slick spots. She was entering more familiar territory as they neared the ranger station.

She kept them away from the main road even as they approached the station. She was tired, parched and starving, but she didn't want to stop. Darkness was approaching and there was no time to stop.

So she told herself. Better than thinking about what she might have to face if they stopped.

Felicity came up short as she saw a figure in the distance. At first she thought it might be another ranger doing rounds, but the figure was wearing a baseball cap, not a park uniform.

"Just keep hiking. Act casual. Normal," Gage instructed. "It might be our ride. It might not be. If she approaches us, just act like you would with any other hiker."

Felicity swallowed at the nerves fluttering in her

throat, but she nodded and kept hiking again. No matter where Felicity and Gage walked, the figure moved so their paths would cross.

When Felicity saw that she was a woman dressed all in black, with no signs of backpacking gear, she prayed to God it was someone from the secret group Cody had worked for last year.

Because if not, it was bad news indeed.

"Howdy," the woman greeted as they finally met on solid ground covered in grass. "Nice evening for a hike, isn't it?"

"Getting a little late," Felicity offered, working hard to keep her voice steady and without stutter.

"It is." The woman tipped her unnecessary sunglasses down. "You guys need a ride?" She jerked her chin in the direction of the road. "You're looking a little worse for wear, and I've got a truck not far off."

Felicity exchanged a glance with Gage.

"Sure, Shay," Gage said.

The woman smiled and winked. "Follow me, Wyatt."

Felicity blew out a breath. It was their ride, thank God. They still had a good mile walk, and exhaustion pounded at her temples. She had no idea what Gage had in mind once they got to her cabin. They'd been through a tornado, and miles and miles of hiking. All she wanted to do was sleep.

Shay led them to a big black truck with tinted windows Felicity doubted were legal. She climbed into the back of the truck anyway, Gage getting into the front seat. Gage and Shay spoke in low tones and Felicity tried to pay attention, but she couldn't stop herself from dozing as the truck began to drive.

She awoke with a start when she realized the vehicle had stopped. Shay and Gage were outside, heads together as they spoke. Felicity looked around. They were in the grove of trees not far from her cabin.

When she pushed the door open and stepped out, Gage and Shay immediately stopped talking.

Felicity frowned at them.

Gage leaned close to Shay and whispered something.

Shay nodded. "Thanks. Good luck." She smiled at Felicity as she walked back to the truck. "Especially for you."

Felicity didn't know what to say to that, but Shay was gone in a flash anyway. "What was that?" she demanded of Gage.

He shrugged, studying the trees. "Don't worry about it."

"Don't worry about… Are you… You can't…"

"Calm it down, Red."

"I'd like to punch you."

"I'd like to see you try," he returned mildly.

She was tempted. She'd convinced Tucker to teach her how to land a decent blow before she'd gone off on her first seasonal park ranger job in Kentucky. But something told her even if she threw a decent jab-cross combo, Gage would never let them land.

"Come on. Let's get to the cabin."

It was dark now, the air cool. Everything felt wrong

and eerie, and she had a flash of the woman's body at the bottom of the canyon.

The woman who was apparently her sister.

She shuddered as they walked as silently as possible. The tornado clearly hadn't been through this way, though a few downed branches suggested some heavy storms. She hoped her cabin hadn't sustained any damage.

When they reached the edge of the trees and she could detect the outline of her cabin in the moonlight, she felt her stomach sink in despair. Not because of damage, though. "There's police tape," she whispered.

"Lucky for you, I'm the police."

"Gage."

He was already striding forward. He went to the back door and began untying one side of the Do Not Cross tape. Felicity stood in the clearing of her cabin and stared, openmouthed. "You can't—"

He cut off her directive. "Come on now. We've left following the rules behind. Keep up, Felicity." He motioned her forward.

SHE STOOD AS if she wasn't going to listen to him. But Gage knew there was no other way right now. Maybe they wouldn't find any leads in her cabin, but it would give them a place to sleep for the night—a place no one would dream of looking for them.

Finally Felicity moved forward.

"Got your keys?"

She didn't answer, just frowned deeper and pulled keys out of her pocket. She unlocked the door and gingerly stepped inside. Gage tied the police tape back to the banister and walked in behind her.

She stood, miserably surveying her tiny kitchen. "They moved things," she said. "Went through my home and…" She shook her head.

He gave her shoulder a squeeze, though it made her jump. Still, he couldn't stand to see that look of utter defeat on her face. She'd gotten through the past forty-eight hours on grit and determination and strength. He knew how hard it was to hold on to that when things seemed bleak.

But she needed to.

"Don't get sad. Get mad, Felicity. Someone came through here and planted evidence against you. The cops are doing their job, and it sucks that's their job, but let's focus on who's trying to make you into a murderer."

She didn't say anything for the longest time. When she finally did, she did it moving toward the fridge. "I'm hungry." She opened it, studied the contents and shook her head. She slammed the door, wrenched open the freezer, then brought out a tub of ice cream.

She grabbed a spoon, settled herself down at the tiny table in the corner and went to work.

"We might want something a little bit more nourishing."

The look she gave him could have melted that ice cream in front of her.

"I do, anyway."

"Help yourself," she said through a mouthful of ice cream, gesturing at the small refrigerator and pantry.

Gage poked around, found some mixed nuts and a beer, and helped himself. Not exactly nourishing, but maybe she was right that comfort food was the way to go tonight. He settled into the chair across from her, wondered if she ever had any cabin guests that necessitated another chair and kept his opinions on that to himself.

He lifted the beer. "You sit around drinking a lot of beer by yourself?"

"Slugs," she replied. "Kills 'em."

He chuckled. He had no earthly understanding of why he found that endearing or why he could so easily picture her putting out little trays of beer for slugs just as Grandma Pauline always had.

"I'm giving myself five minutes to wallow," she said, scooping up another large glob of ice cream. "I survived a tornado. I'm wanted for murder. A murder I didn't commit. You…" She trailed off before she finished that sentence. "I get five minutes to wallow." She shoved the entire bite of ice cream in her mouth.

"Then what?"

She swallowed and looked down at the container. "I don't know."

"I tell you what. Let's extend the wallow. Ten minutes with the ice cream, then about—" he checked the clock on his phone "—five hours of sleep in a bed."

"Then what?" she asked, echoing his own question back to him.

"In the morning, we check in with my brothers and see if they've made any progress or have any idea where Ace is. We'll go through your cabin and see if we can find anything off or missing. Then…I want to go look at where you found the body."

She shoved away from the table, abruptly sticking the lid on the ice cream and putting it back in the freezer.

"Felici—"

She whirled to face him. "Tell me one of your stories."

"Huh?"

"Those crazy stories you pull out whenever everyone's down and you want to get a laugh." She pointed to herself. "I'm depressed." Then to him. "Now, cheer me up. Make me laugh."

"I can't do it on command."

"Why not?"

"Well, for starters, it's not what you need right now."

"Oh, really. What do I need?"

He stood. He could do without the beer and they'd have a chance to eat in the morning, so he left both on the table. He walked over to her and, as gratifying as it was that her eyes got wide and dropped to his mouth, he didn't do what she was clearly expecting him to.

He simply wrapped his arms around her and gave her a squeeze. "We need sleep," he said. Much as he wanted to hold her a little closer, stroke a lot more than her hair, it wasn't the time.

He pulled back from the friendly hug and she blinked up at him. "I guess you're right," she said at length. "I have extra sheets for the couch."

He snorted out a laugh, which he tried to bite back when she glared at him. "Bad news. We've still got to be careful. We'll want to be out of here before sunrise, and we need to be close. No separate rooms, Felicity."

"Just what are you suggesting?"

"I'm not *suggesting* anything. We're going to have to sleep in the same place. Whether it's your couch or your bed, you've got a sleeping buddy tonight. So, pick your poison. My guess is your bed has more room."

"You're not going to sleep in *my* bed. With *me*," she returned, all shrieking outrage.

Gage didn't figure arguing with her was going to get him anywhere, so he shrugged and headed for the door he was pretty sure led to her bedroom. She scurried after him, blustering without forming any actual words.

He opened the door, walked over to the bed, toed off his boots, gave her a look that said *try and stop me* and settled himself onto one side.

She stood there and stared at him, mouth open, little sounds of outrage escaping.

God, he was too tired for her outrage. "You can tie me up if it'd make you more comfortable. Might give me some ideas, but if it'd make you feel better, be my guest."

She scowled at him. "I'm not *afraid* of you."

She certainly seemed it. Well, maybe *afraid* was harsh. She was nervous. Jumpy and high-strung— keeping as much space between her and him sprawled out on the bed as possible.

"Want to talk about earlier first?" He couldn't say he particularly *wanted* to talk about that kiss, but it was muddling his mind when he needed to be lucid and think about how on earth they were going to clear her.

"No!" she squeaked.

The squeak amused him even if it shouldn't. "Suit yourself."

"Fine. *I'll* sleep on the couch."

"No, you won't, Felicity. You're in here with me, if I have to tie *you* up." He might have ended it on a joke, but he was deadly serious and she seemed to understand that.

After huffing and crossing her arms over her chest, then throwing them up in the air a second later, she finally stalked to the bed. She wrenched off her boots, muttering the whole time, then lowered herself onto the bed.

In Gage's estimation, the full-size mattress was hardly adequate for one person let alone two.

No matter, she was putting as much space between them as if they were on a king-size.

It was dark in here, but it smelled like her. And if she thought *she* was ticked off about the sleeping arrangements, she had *no* idea what was going through his head.

He was almost asleep when she finally spoke.

"You kissed me," she said, as if it was some grave accusation.

"That I did." And he didn't regret it in the slightest, even if she hated him for it. She'd kissed him back.

Him. Not Brady. There might be a little sibling jealousy there, but when he'd said he wasn't Brady earlier she'd looked so shocked he had to believe she hadn't been thinking about Brady when she'd kissed him back.

"Why did you do it?" she asked, her voice soft, and he would have said *timid* if he didn't know how damn strong she was.

"Because I wanted to."

"That's hardly an answer."

"Why?"

"Because you don't just suddenly want to kiss someone after never wanting to kiss them."

"Who said I never wanted to?"

She was quiet at that, so he rolled onto his side with an exaggerated yawn. "Night, Felicity."

She didn't respond, and he fell off into a deep sleep.

HE AWOKE TO something vibrating against him and realized it was his phone.

He swore internally when he saw it was four in the morning, but it was a text from Jamison: Call ASAP.

He slid out of the bed, tempted to spend a little too much time staring at Felicity in the glow from his phone. She was still dead asleep, face relaxed, hair a mess around her head.

Prettiest damn thing he'd ever seen, and he did not have time to dwell on this too-soft feeling going on inside of him.

He moved into the living room and called Jamison. "What do you have?"

Jamison didn't waste time or words. "Prints came back last night—one of Tuck's friends sent him an email. Tuck just got off another case and called me." Jamison was in full cop mode, and Gage didn't interrupt. "They found Felicity's biological father's prints on the evidence they sent for DNA testing. They'd also found his prints in her cabin. Tucker's going to go talk to the detectives this morning, explain that Felicity hasn't had a thing to do with her father so this is unusual. With the tornado damage, Felicity isn't high on their list of priorities—which is good and bad. Good, you guys should be able to remain undetected. Bad, they're not going to worry about dropping the warrant yet."

"Her father had something to do with it?"

"It's looking that way to me. Added to that? He's disappeared since the tornado, and I doubt he's a casualty."

"Why do you doubt that?"

"We've done some digging. The real reason I called you. There's something bigger at play."

"Something bigger than someone framing Felicity for murder?"

"Bigger or more connected anyway. Gage, Michael Harrison visited Ace in jail. Before the murder."

"How? We've been tracking that."

"He signed in to speak to another prisoner, but after looking deeper into it, there was a switch and he managed to talk to Ace thanks to a paid-off guard."

Gage let that sink in. Felicity's biological father had visited Ace in jail. His father and hers were connected.

And he had no doubt his father was behind it all.

Chapter Ten

Felicity had never been a particularly good sleeper. Night terrors had plagued her as a kid, and while she'd grown out of those for the most part, vivid dreams still afflicted her often. Not always bad ones, just clear and real-feeling.

She opened her eyes, her body hot and heart racing, more than a little embarrassed at just *what* her vivid imagination had been up to. Steeling herself, she turned her head, but Gage wasn't there.

She told herself she was relieved, even blew out a breath as if to convince herself she was. But some echo of the dream was still thrumming inside of her and at the center of that thrumming she was most definitely not relieved.

Then from somewhere outside the room she heard Gage swear, quietly but in an uncharacteristically serious tone she knew meant bad news.

There was no rest from the true, important, pressing issues in their lives. But the words that rattled around in her head as she slid out of bed weren't anything to do with being accused of murder or Ace being on the loose.

It was Gage's voice, grave and completely unflinching, saying *because I wanted to* over and over again.

She didn't have to work to silence that voice when she stepped out to the living room, though. Gage turned to face her. The pure gentleness in his look might have totally undone her if it didn't scare her to the bone.

"What is it?"

"Why don't you have a seat?"

"What is it?" she returned, trying to do his one-eyebrow quirk.

He didn't say anything. She wasn't sure he even breathed, which made it very hard for her to.

"Jamison and Tucker have been busy," he said, with a hesitance in his voice that felt very un-Gage-like and even more disconcerting. "Looking into things and... there are things."

"Be specific, Gage."

"They found your father's prints in the cabin and on the evidence."

Felicity wished she'd taken that seat he'd wanted her to. "I don't understand."

"No one does, just yet. But I assume you haven't been entertaining your father here?"

"Here? Entertaining? I haven't had any contact with my father since Child Protection Services took me away." She crossed her arms over herself, trying to keep all the awful parts of that sentence tightly under her control instead of at the will of her emotion.

"That's what I thought. Well, he was here. Your father was *in* your cabin at some point."

"That's… If he was here, he planted the evidence." Which meant he could be the killer. Why would he kill his own child? He'd beaten Felicity herself when she'd been helpless and small, and still she had a hard time wrapping her mind around the possibility he'd gone so far as to end his own child's life. "He planted the evidence?"

"That's the angle Tucker is going to press upon the detectives, and at least that there's no good reason his prints should be here. But with the tornado, everyone's busy. This case has fallen in priority."

"My father was here?" Why would he… After all this time, why would he be causing her trouble now? And such awful, horrible trouble. She wrapped her arms around herself, trying to find some center of fight or determination when all she felt was unaccountably sad.

That's when she realized Gage remained very still, watching her with a dark hazel gaze that looked pained. "There's more." She didn't even have to put it as a question. She knew. There was more.

Exhaustion threatened despite the sleep. This was life exhaustion. This was how many blows could one person take and keep going.

The answer was always *as many as life hands you*, but that answer sincerely sucked right now.

"Jamison found out…" He cleared his throat. "Michael Harrison went to visit Ace before you found the body."

Felicity had never fainted in her life, but the room spun and faded to black and her knees went to jelly. Before she could collapse, Gage was at her side, his strong arm around her waist leading her to the couch.

Her father and Ace? It made a horrible, terrifying kind of sense. This wasn't isolated. It wasn't just her father or just Ace. It was them together. Why were Ace and her father acting together?

Gage crouched in front of her, but she didn't know what to say to him. All she really wanted to do was press her forehead into her knees and cry.

She'd cried enough. She'd wallowed enough.

But how did she keep going forward knowing that it wasn't just Ace against her, it was her own father. That the life of a woman—a sister she'd never known—was over because of her in some warped, weird way.

"You can't start blaming yourself," Gage said sharply, as if he could read her thoughts.

"You don't know what it's like to have a father who…" She trailed off and mentally kicked herself.

"Don't know what it's like to have an evil murderer for a father?" He made a considering noise. "It just so happens I know a thing or two about that."

"I don't. I never thought my father was *that* bad." There'd only been four years. Years she didn't fully remember.

"He beat you," Gage said flatly.

"I know, but…" She didn't know how the next words came out, when this was Gage, not her therapist and not her sister. But Gage. And still, the words tumbled into the silence. "Sometimes you have to… I had to tell myself it was just a bad temper. I had to tell myself it was just bad luck, extraordinary circumstances that made him snap. I couldn't make him the bad guy because what did that make me?" She realized, again, that was the worst thing to say when she looked up at him and there was a kind of desolation on his face.

Because he knew. He understood. All those feelings she'd never been able to fully articulate in the therapy Eva had made her go to when she'd first been with the Knights, when she'd talked with Nina or Liza about their less-than-stellar childhoods. She didn't even have to articulate it for it to make sense to Gage.

Suddenly she had to know, to fully understand, the breadth and width of Ace Wyatt. "Did Ace hit all of you?"

"Yeah."

"And worse?"

"I don't know how to quantify worse, Felicity." He raked a hand through his hair, a rare sign of discomfort and frustration. "It was only eleven years."

"He abandoned you in the elements when you were seven as some kind of initiation."

"Yeah. But see, I only had five years of that. Jamison? He did thirteen. Each year it went up one."

"Went up one?" She could tell he didn't want to say more, that he'd already said more than he wanted to, but she needed understanding. For both of them. "Please, Gage."

"You stayed on your own one night for every year of life. It wasn't so bad. It was a week plus without Ace. Without those people. Maybe it was hard to find food and water. Maybe..." He shook his head, as if to shake it all away. "It was awful. But it was all awful. Beatings, whippings, initiations. Trying to pit us against each other. He's a terrifying man. A sociopath with a deep understanding of people—how to manipulate them, inspire them, twist them."

She didn't know how she understood him. What he spoke of was longer, truly more awful than her four sketchy years under her father's care. But she understood that he worried what all that twisting had done to him, no matter how hard he'd tried to fight it. She reached out and touched his cheek on the side of his face that wasn't bandaged. "He didn't twist his sons."

The look of anguish on his face, as if he wasn't so sure, just about broke her heart. "You're good men," she insisted. "Regardless of what our fathers are— evil sociopaths and murderers or what all—it doesn't matter. We're good." She took his large, rough hands and squeezed as hard as she could. "I know we are."

He looked at their joined hands, then up at her. He had a heartbreaking look in his eyes, as if he was the personal cause for everything bad that had ever happened.

"I hate that you're on his radar, because this will hurt. Even when we win, this will hurt."

She couldn't help feeling some bubble of hope, the curve of a smile. "*When* we win?"

"We're not going to lose, Felicity. I won't let it happen. Whatever it takes."

She had no cause to doubt him, because they'd gotten through this far. But she understood in that vehe-

ment promise, that Gage cared. Not just about himself.
Not just about winning against Ace. But about her.
Period.

She leaned forward and pressed her mouth to his. It
was nothing like the kiss in the Badlands. She was too
shy for that. Didn't know how to lead and run with all
that wild heat. But she kissed him anyway, with what
little skill she had. And he let her—he didn't lead her
anywhere else, just kissed her back as gently and carefully as she'd kissed him.

When she pulled back, he didn't say anything. He
stared, and nerves crept in to dismantle all that surety
about him caring, about him wanting to kiss her for a
lot longer than she'd ever thought of kissing him. "You
said you wanted to kiss me."

"Yeah." He reached out, rubbed a strand of her
hair between his thumb and forefinger. His mouth
was curved, not in a full-blown smile, because even
here there wasn't anything to smile about. But it was
softer than *whatever it takes*. He looked from her hair
to her eyes. "I like kissing you," he said so seriously,
so simply, she couldn't do anything other than believe
it was the truth.

"I think I like it, too." More than anything as simple
as *like*. And it centered her, reminded her that outside
all of this terrifying situation, she had a real life. Was
a woman. Maybe even a woman who ended up kissing Gage Wyatt as much as she pleased. But she had
to fight for that possibility first.

She was ready. She had to find a way to be ready.
"All right. What's the plan now?"

GAGE SUPPOSED STAYING here and taking her to bed wasn't much of a plan when their murderous fathers were on the loose, Felicity their target.

But it was tempting.

Sadly, time wasn't on their side.

"First things first. It's nearing dawn and we've got to clear out in case any detectives stop by. I want to take a look at where the woman's body was. See if we can find any clues of our own."

Felicity winced, but she nodded.

"You don't have to—"

"I'll go with. Two people searching for clues is better than one. I guess it's just that she was my sister. I can't fully grasp it. When I try to think about it, when I try not to think about it. I don't know how to feel."

"You didn't know she existed, Felicity. I'd give yourself a break on that, and if you don't want to relive it, you don't have to."

She shook her head, her hands still in his. It was a nice weight, a sign of partnership, of some level of caring about each other.

It wasn't the time or place to delve into how much, but there was a nice certainty to being in this together.

"We shouldn't be apart. Not with Ace on the loose. Don't you think it's dangerous with him out there?"

He hated that she was right. "He wouldn't necessarily know we're here—I don't know how he could—but you're right. We should stick together. Keep an eye on each other until we know more." Letting her out of his sight wasn't an option.

"So, it's a promise. We stick together, no matter what?"

He nodded. "It's a promise."

She squeezed his hands and then released them. Her face was all determination now—the sadness and fear buried. She stood and slapped her palms on her thighs as if to say *let's go*. "I'll grab my own pack from here. You can carry the one I had. We really should arrange for someone to pick up what we left behind after the tornado."

He didn't know why her stubborn insistence on park protocol warmed his heart like it was damn Christmas or something, but it did.

"Is there an anonymous way to let a ranger know? Hey, maybe it'd even get Ace thinking we're dead. We could have been blown away in the tornado, shattered who knows where, and all that's left is the backpack we dropped."

"What an awful thought." She shuddered. "I guess it'll be okay another few days. Go get the other pack. Grab what might work in my pantry. Load up on water. Water is most important. I'll pack mine with camping gear and bandages and disinfectant so we can keep your wound clean. That should see us through another few days if we have to."

"You didn't ask me what's next after we check out the murder site," he said, slowly standing.

She looked up at him, eyes so green and serious. "We'll go to Sons territory, of course. Ace likely went there. If my father is working for him, or they're working together—they're probably there right now. Maybe not. I don't know them, don't understand them, but we go where their power is. Regardless of whether they're with the Sons or not, someone in the Sons knows something. That's where we have to go."

"That doesn't scare you?"

"It terrifies me. But so does prison. I want to act. I don't want my fight left up to someone else. What other options are there?"

The only one he could think of involved locking her up far away, and he knew she'd never go for that. "We could just hide until Jamison and Cody figure it out."

She actually rolled her eyes as if this wasn't life and death they were talking about. "As if you could stay sane waiting for your brothers to handle everything for you. For *me*, actually. This is my mess. I'm glad you're here with me. I couldn't do it on my own, but it is my mess."

"A mess you're in because Cody called you for help."

"My father—"

"Are we really going to stand here and argue who's more to blame for a mess created by our fathers?"

"Fair point. All right. Pack up."

They went in opposite directions—her to her room, him to the kitchen. He focused on the practicalities, food and water, and trusted her to take care of shelter.

If he entertained himself by thinking of sharing a tent again, well, a man deserved some distraction from all the garbage heaped on him.

She returned to the kitchen, a pack already strapped to her body. She was wearing new khaki pants and a tan sweatshirt that would often blend right in with the landscape they'd be hiking.

She held out a similarly colored lump of clothing. "It won't help with your jeans, but it's an extra large. You don't have to wear it just yet, but it's a good idea to have. Tie it around your waist."

"Men do not *tie* sweatshirts around their waists."

She raised an eyebrow at him. He was not amused at her mimicking him. When he didn't take the sweatshirt at first, she shoved it at him.

"Take a hit on your manliness, Gage. For the sake of—oh, I don't know—surviving, maybe."

He scowled as he took the sweatshirt and tied it around his waist. "Happy?"

"Downright celebratory. Woo-hoo, time to inspect a murder scene!"

Her sarcasm cheered him even if it was at his expense. "Ready to head out?"

She nodded, and though he could see the nerves in her eyes, her hands were steady. Her expression was determined in spite of the fear.

"Oh, one thing first," she said, her expression grave as she walked toward him. She stopped in front of him, looking up at him as if he was supposed to have an idea what that one thing was.

Then she put her hands on his shoulders, rose to her toes and pressed a kiss to his mouth. It was soft, a little timid like the one in the living room, but sweet. And sweet was just as potent as anything else when it came to her.

She lowered back to flat-footed. Her cheeks were

edging toward red, but her smile was satisfied even if she was embarrassed, too.

If he didn't die from Ace, he might from this.

He wanted to tell her…everything. How watching her change and find her strength had shifted something inside of him. Had set a spark to this feeling he didn't quite understand. Something bigger than himself and the fear of being Ace Wyatt's son.

He didn't have the words for any of that. So, he grinned at her and then made a move for the back door. He stepped out, his mind still fuzzy with *feelings* he didn't know how to verbalize.

He heard a shuffle, but before he could react, the cold press of steel was at his temple and his father's amused voice in his ear.

"Well, hello, son. Funny running into you here."

Chapter Eleven

Felicity tried to scramble back and run in the opposite direction, but Ace was too quick. His arm snaked in and grabbed her by the shirtfront.

"Not so fast." Ace laughed and the sound made her stomach turn in utter terror.

She wanted to fight him, but the gun pressed to Gage's temple kept her frozen in fear. Even if he didn't want to kill his own son, any struggling from her could have him pulling the trigger—purposefully or accidentally.

Then there was her own father standing in the yard, a much larger gun than Ace's slung over his arm. She hadn't seen him in years, didn't recognize him on a visual level, but she knew it was him.

Ace gave her shirt a jerk, sending her pitching forward. The weight of the backpack added to her inelegant loss of balance, and she landed hard on the ground. She struggled to get up. Maybe she could run for help? But that would leave Gage here. Alone with them.

Her father moved close and stood over her. He didn't

press the gun to her temple like Ace had his to Gage, but he pointed it at her all the same.

"Can you believe it, son?" Ace was saying to Gage, grinning from ear to ear even with a gun pressed to his own son's temple. "A tornado busted me out of jail. A *tornado*. Can you understand the absolute significance of that divine intervention?"

"I'm sure you'll enlighten me whether I want you to or not."

"When my parents left me to die, it was the land that protected me, built me. Now it's the land, the fearsome power of this land, that's given me my freedom back after my sons were too weak, too soft to do what they were meant to do."

Felicity shuddered at the words, at how reasonable they sounded to her. She understood what it felt like to be made new by the awe-inspiring landscape around them. The preacher-like way he spoke those words had her listening, rapt. Understanding.

She had something in common with Ace Wyatt. What a horrible, horrible thought.

"You think it's a weakness not to be you, Ace. But you're outnumbered, because the sane ones among us consider it a strength to be able to battle back our worst impulses. To not believe ourselves the ultimate judge, jury and executioner."

Ace cocked his head as he studied Gage. "A nice story you six have told yourselves. But there are six of you. One of you will have to face the music. Or the end will come."

"Endings always come. And the most poetic end-ing for you will be rotting in a cell for the rest of your insane life."

"The land provides. It provides the willing and the worthy, and it has provided me my freedom, again."

He sounded so rational, so utterly sure, Felicity had to remind herself he *was* insane. Evil, surely, if he'd killed people and done some of the things the Wyatts said he did.

"Then, after the land anoints me yet again, frees. and provides and gives to me, *yet again*, I'm lucky enough to stumble upon exactly who I was figuring out how to find."

"I thought you didn't believe in luck," Gage said, his voice cool and detached as if a deadly weapon wasn't pressed to his head.

Ace chuckled. "Oh, I believe in it. I also believe it favors the prepared and anointed. I am both. What are you?"

Gage muttered disparagingly under his breath. He was staring straight ahead so he couldn't see the way Ace's eyes gleamed.

Crazy. Evil. Felicity didn't know what it was, but that sheen made everything inside of her ice, made the hair on her arms and back of her neck stand up on end. All that reason she'd almost thought he'd been speaking evaporated when she looked at him.

She focused on breathing evenly in an effort to keep panic at bay. She had to find a way to survive this. A way for both of them to survive their fathers.

There wasn't much that could be done with Ace

holding a gun to Gage's head and her father pointing a gun at her.

Don't panic. Don't panic. Think.

The Wyatt brothers had always said their father didn't want them dead, or they'd be dead. There were multiple theories, though most centered on the idea Ace Wyatt wanted slow, painful revenge on his sons, not just a violent death.

The likelihood of Ace actually pulling the trigger was low. And since neither had shot her, maybe they didn't want her dead, either.

Still, she could visualize Ace shooting Gage—see it happening before her, and that kept her from moving. From hoping.

Two against two might have been a fair fight if she had a weapon of her own, but all she had was a backpacking knife stuffed deep within the pack on her back. Was there any way to get it without drawing attention to herself? And even if there was, what was the point of bringing a knife to a gunfight?

"I don't know what brand-new break you've had with reality," Gage drawled, "but—"

Ace's free hand jabbed out so fast Felicity barely saw it. She wasn't even sure where the punch landed, only that it had Gage gasping for air and falling to his knees.

"You weren't next on my list, Gage. But you mixed yourself up with this one and messed up my plan. You know how I feel when people mess up my plan."

The only thing that came from Gage was horrible gasping noises as if he was struggling to breathe.

Without fully realizing she was doing it, she moved toward him. Until an excruciating pain in her hand stopped her. She looked at the source of the crushing, terrifying pain and found her father's boot pressing harder and harder against her hand.

"You stay put," he said.

She tried not to sob, not to react, but he ground the boot harder against her hand. He was going to break her fingers with much more pressure. The only thing currently saving her was the give of the soil after the rain.

"Got it?" he demanded, jabbing her side with his gun.

She nodded, tears streaming down her cheeks. But she didn't make a noise.

The pressure eased off her hand, and she wanted to sob with as much relief as throbbing pain, but she breathed through it.

"Felicity, I need you to break your promise to me," Gage said, his voice clear and calm, which earned him another punch from Ace, right against the throat.

Her promise? Her promise. To stay together no matter what. No. No, she couldn't break it. She couldn't leave him here.

But as he gasped for air against his father's horrifying blows, she realized that in this case, splitting up was the only chance they had. Ace would have somewhere to take them, somewhere to torture them.

If she could get away, she could get all the Wyatts here. She could save Gage. She didn't want to leave him with Ace, even for a second. But when they'd promised each other to stick together that had been when

Ace was out there. When the threat was from the outside, not the inside.

She couldn't save Gage with brute strength, but if she could get away she might be able to save him some other way.

She met his gaze. And nodded.

GAGE DIDN'T LET the nerves show, didn't let on how afraid he was because God knew this was going to hurt.

But she'd be safe—or safer. It was the only chance he had to survive. Maybe he wouldn't, but if she was safe that would be okay.

So, he had to make sure he did enough damage to Ace that Michael came over to save him. He had to give Felicity enough time to really run.

The two men holding guns on them would kill her, no doubt. They'd kill him, too, but Ace would want to make it hurt first. Maybe he'd want it to hurt for Felicity, too, since she'd gotten in Ace's way with Nina and Cody, but that only made her being here, in their grasp, that much more dangerous.

"Have you had your dramatic mom—"

Gage interrupted his father's comment by throwing his head backward, and straight into his father's.

It rang his bell—stars dancing and pain radiating down to his toes, but the gun dropped from his temple. Gage took the opportunity to pitch his body forward hoping his legs would hold him.

He still had the damn pack on his back and wished he'd had the foresight to drop it, but when Michael came charging at him, Gage managed to get an arm out of the strap and use it as enough of a force to knock the gun pointed at him from Michael's hands.

Gage didn't stop to look and see if Felicity ran. There wasn't time for him to look, so he just had to trust that she'd understood him and that she'd nodded because she knew she was going to run.

Michael swore at him and charged.

Felicity's father did not appear to be the smartest man, but he had fists like mallets, and was all bulk and muscle. Though he'd lost his gun, he used his body as a weapon against Gage, landing two punches to the gut before Gage could block them.

Gage was not a small man, but he felt like one for a second. Michael making him feel small only reminded him that Felicity had been small. A tiny girl and this man had used his fists on her—enough that protective services had intervened—which was a bit of a feat in isolated rural areas with low government funds.

Gage used that rage, that utter disgust to propel him forward with a blow that knocked Michael back two steps.

A gunshot rang out too close, but no blast of pain followed the noise. Still, Gage knew well enough Ace wouldn't miss twice. Even to forward his precious plans.

So Gage grappled with Michael, finally landing a knee to the most vulnerable part of his attacker. He managed to flip him off and then got to his feet, only to come face-to-face with Ace's gun barrel.

"Well, shoot me then," Gage snarled. His mouth was bleeding, and God knew what other parts of him were bleeding and broken. Every cell of his body hurt, and this was all so pointless.

Not pointless. Felicity is gone. He didn't dare look around and verify. He just *willed* it.

Ace's own face was bleeding, and Gage got morbid satisfaction from knowing his head had caused that gash on Ace's brow.

Ace's gaze whipped behind Michael, from the gun that had fallen to the ground, to the pack that had been ripped from Gage's back.

"You let her *go*?" Ace growled.

Michael was struggling to get to his feet. "He practically knocked you out. I had to—"

"You worthless moron! Go after her! Go!"

Gage couldn't help smiling even as blood dripped down his face. He wasn't sure he'd ever heard Ace sound so furiously disgusted. Usually his anger was deadly, eerie calm, but Gage had clearly put quite the crimp in Ace's plans.

Who wouldn't grin at that? Especially as Michael scrambled to retrieve the gun and then ran off more in panic than with any thought as to which way Felicity had gone.

She'd be faster and far more knowledgeable of the terrain. She was gone and on her way to find help. Gage had to believe it.

"What are you smiling ab…" Ace trailed off, rage and disgust sinking into the lines on his face.

"Jail didn't agree with you, Daddy," Gage offered, hoping to throw Ace off.

"You care about her." Ace sneered. "What is it about

you boys? Where did I go so wrong? Weak. Stupid. Undone by any woman who opens her legs."

Gage couldn't keep the easy grin on his face, and it morphed into a sneer. But he bit his tongue to keep from saying anything that might give Ace more ammunition to rail against and agitate Gage into making a deadly misstep.

"What a mistake you've made," Ace whispered, a vicious fury dancing in his eyes, that Gage only remembered seeing once before—when Ace had realized Cody had escaped.

Jamison had worked hard to get Cody, the youngest of the six boys, out from the Sons before he had to go through the ritual they'd all had to survive on their seventh birthdays. Jamison had managed, managed so well Ace had assumed Grandma Pauline had paid one of his men to betray him. He'd never suspected Jamison.

At first.

That moment Ace had learned Cody was safe and out of his grip, Gage had seen this exact look. And known he'd be lucky to survive it.

But he had then, why couldn't he now?

Which was the last thought he had before pain exploded at the side of his head, and the world went dark.

One Minute" Survey

You get up to **FOUR books** <u>and</u> TWO Mystery Gifts...

YOU pick your books –
WE pay for everything.
You get up to FOUR new books and TWO Mystery Gift.
absolutely FREE!
Total retail value: Over $20!

Dear Reader,

Your opinions are important to us. So if you'll participate in our fa
and free "One Minute" Survey, **YOU** can pick up to four wonderfu
books that **WE** pay for!

As a leading publisher of women's fiction, we'd love to hear from
you. That's why we promise to reward you for completing our
survey.

IMPORTANT: Please complete the survey and return it. We'll sen
your Free Books and Free Mystery Gifts right away. **And we pay
for shipping and handling too!** ← *We pay for EVERYTHING!*

Try **Harlequin® Romantic Suspense** books featuring heart-racing
page-turners with unexpected plot twists and irresistible chemist
that will keep you guessing to the very end.

Try **Harlequin Intrigue® Larger-Print** books featuring action-pack
stories that will keep you on the edge of your seat. Solve the crim
and deliver justice at all costs.

Or TRY BOTH!

Thank you again for participating in our "One Minute"
Survey. It really takes just a minute (or less) to complete the
survey… and your free books and gifts will be well worth it!

Sincerely,

Pam Powers

Pam Powers
for Reader Service

"One Minute" Survey

GET YOUR FREE BOOKS AND FREE GIFTS!

✓ Complete this Survey   ✓ Return this survey

1   Do you try to find time to read every day?

☐ YES   ☐ NO

2   Do you prefer stories with suspenseful storylines?

☐ YES   ☐ NO

3   Do you enjoy having books delivered to your home?

☐ YES   ☐ NO

4   Do you find a Larger Print size easier on your eyes?

☐ YES   ☐ NO

YES! I have completed the above "One Minute" Survey. Please send me my Free Books and Free Mystery Gifts (worth over $20 retail). I understand that I am under no obligation to buy anything, as explained on the back of this card.

☐ I prefer Harlequin® Romantic Suspense 240/340 HDL GNUS

☐ I prefer Harlequin® Intrigue® Larger Print 199/399 HDL GNUS

☐ I prefer BOTH 240/340 & 199/399 HDL GNWG

FIRST NAME   LAST NAME

ADDRESS

APT.#   CITY

STATE/PROV.   ZIP/POSTAL CODE

Chapter Twelve

Felicity tried to keep her mind off the lack of water. Once she found cell service, she'd have help and water.

Her head pounded along with her thundering heart. She knew she could outrun her father, but he had a gun, which meant she had to do a lot more than just outrun him. She had to get away completely.

Now, Ace, he could probably catch her if he was the one chasing her. Her father was a big man, and though she remembered a certain agile precision in landing a blow, she doubted it extended to endurance running.

But Ace was tall and lean and crazy. That was the worst part, really. He seemed almost normal sometimes. She'd found herself listening too intently to what he had to say.

Charismatic wasn't the right word because that had too positive of a connotation. Compelling maybe. Even knowing everything she did about Ace—which was probably only the half of what Ace was and had done— she'd been *compelled* to listen to what he had to say.

It made her feel sick. Or maybe that was the dehydration.

She allowed her pace to slow, then stop, turning in a careful circle to study her surroundings.

She'd gone straight for the canyon land, which may not have been her smartest choice what with the lack of water, but it was better than the wide-open grassy plains. There were a million places to find cover in the rocks, crevices and caves.

And that was only if her father found her.

She was currently in a long, deep crevice. Some of the wet from yesterday's storm had dried, but there were still damp places where the sun hadn't touched. Not safe drinking water, but she considered it for a minute.

Maybe she should go back. Knife in hand. They weren't supposed to split up. This was all wrong.

She climbed up a portion of the rock wall that would allow her to see out over the horizon while still keeping her mostly out of sight. She scanned the area, the tall spires and rocky hills. The sky was a brilliant blue, as if a tornado hadn't blown through less than twenty-four hours ago.

The air was hot, but it was *Badlands* air. Home. Heart. She'd be okay.

The land provides.

The thought comforted her for a second or two before she realized it was Ace's voice. Ace's words.

She pushed out a breath, nausea stealing over her. How could a madman's words be comforting? Had she gone crazy? Was she that weak?

She shook her head. Maybe she was, but she could choose not to be. She could fight it. It was like being shy, and her stutter. Those things still existed within her, but she fought them away.

So she would fight the terrifying idea she had something in common with Ace Wyatt. Just as for years she'd fought the terrifying idea a man who'd beat his young daughter was her own flesh and blood.

And that flesh and blood had come after her, no doubt. She looked around again, a double check to make sure her eyes weren't deceiving her.

She caught the hint of movement to the east and squinted at it. Then, since she had time, she dug through her pack and pulled out her binoculars. She focused on the area where she'd sensed movement.

In between two spindly spires of red rock, a figure was moving. He was still far enough away the binoculars didn't magnify features enough for identification, but based on the size and location, she had to believe it was her father.

He didn't look like an adept hiker. He stumbled and picked his way over rock. She could continue to outrun or out-hike him if she chose.

But she would no doubt become too dehydrated to function after a while.

What were her options? He had a gun and he was clearly stronger than her. She couldn't fight him. She had no gun to ward him off. Just that knife in her pack.

She considered waiting till he got close enough and then throwing it, but she'd never thrown a knife in her life and it seemed too big a risk to just start throwing her one and only weapon.

Rocks might work. She was strong and had good

aim, but he'd have to be really close for them to do any damage.

She kept watching him through the binoculars. Maybe she wouldn't have to do anything at all. One good fall and he'd be out of luck.

One good fall. What if she *created* the fall? She could take him out. Even with him having a gun, all she'd need to do was give him a little push. Well, more than a little, but a push. Or trip him somehow. She could incapacitate him or trap him in a deep crevice.

It would be tricky and dangerous, but it would be a better option than trying to find cell service without any water to drink. If she took out her father here, she could get back to the cabin. Close enough to it and she could access her Wi-Fi and send a text.

If she was careful and quiet, she could do it without Ace even knowing she was back. Surely he wouldn't take Gage anywhere until her father returned with her in tow.

She'd hope, anyway.

In the meantime, she'd take her father out.

THE PAIN EBBED and flowed, excruciating waves of it, dulling into something almost bearable. Almost reasonable enough he could fight through, open his eyes and figure everything out.

Then another wave would take him under. Black, black, vicious black.

But then something happened, a familiar sound, a familiar panic. He found consciousness gasping for air and eyes flying open. His vision swam for a good few seconds before it cleared.

And there was Ace.

With the whip.

Gage tried to remember he wasn't seven years old any longer. He was an adult. Whatever his father could dish out, he could take.

But that whip was the nightmare he thought he'd escaped. He wouldn't let those old memories rush into his brain. There was enough pain there. He had to focus on the present. Where he was and if Michael was here—because if he wasn't, he was still somewhere after Felicity.

Felicity. He'd focus on her and not the echoing crack of that whip.

"Good morning, son. Or should I say, good afternoon?"

Gage didn't say anything, though he wanted to demand to know how long he'd been out. He wanted to demand a whole myriad of things, but he didn't trust his voice with that whip in his father's hands.

Ace shifted it from one hand to another. "Did you think I'd forgotten? You never forget your son's weaknesses." Ace smiled, a grin that was all sharp edges and sure as hell crazy.

Except Ace always knew what he was doing. So maybe he was just evil. Maybe all his talk about being anointed and chosen and born from the dust were the things he used to justify all that potential for horror he had inside him.

Gage had never really cared to find out. Especially when that whip was involved.

He wasn't a child anymore. He was *not* a child anymore. The whip would hurt, but it couldn't break him. He couldn't let it. That was what his father wanted, so he wouldn't give it to him.

But his body wasn't getting the message. There was the nausea, which he could blame on the concussion he had to have been given. The heart-pounding, sweaty-palmed terror making his limbs weak—that was all whip.

It's just a weapon like any other.

But it wasn't. Not for him.

"Why do you get the whip, Gage?"

Gage wouldn't respond. He wouldn't. He didn't have to give in. Not anymore. This wasn't the same game it had been when he'd been a defenseless boy.

Maybe he was tied up in what appeared to be some kind of cave...always a cave. But he was thirty-one years old. A grown man who'd fought drug addicts and arrested child molesters and done what he could, *everything* he could, to right the wrongs he came across.

He had to survive this wrong. He'd done it once, much younger but with his brothers' help.

Now he was an adult, and if Felicity had gotten away, it could be with his brothers' help again.

If Felicity and his brothers could find him.

Big, *big* if.

Ace stepped forward, still moving the whip handle from hand to hand.

"The rules are the same, boy."

Gage shuddered as if he was still that little boy. As if the years meant nothing. His size meant nothing. There was Ace and that whip, and Gage was nothing in its wake.

No.

"I ask a question, you answer it. Why do you get the whip?"

"Because my father's a psychopath?"

The crack slammed through the air the same time the stinging, breath-stealing pain lashed over his leg. He couldn't hold back the hiss of pain, despite knowing it was exactly what his father wanted.

It would be worse—get worse. His father's whip was weighted and could break bones with the right slap.

Gage could survive it. Better to survive it than give in like he'd had to as a kid.

"Why do you get the whip, Gage? You and no one else?" Ace cracked the whip between them, and though Gage cringed at the sound, no blast of pain followed it.

Psychological warfare. It wasn't enough to just hurt his sons—he wanted to break them. The problem was, if you were broken, the pain would stop.

For a time, but the war never stopped. There would always be this war between Ace and his sons, because they'd dared to be good instead of capitulate to his evil.

He'd promised himself never to be weak in the face of his father again. But giving Ace what he wanted without truly believing it wasn't weakness. It was survival.

What wouldn't Gage do to survive? To make sure Felicity had survived?

"I get the whip because I'm the smartest," Gage said, his voice already battle weary.

"Good," Ace replied in the same tone a teacher might use when a student finally succeeded with a difficult concept.

It made Gage feel slimy, slick with self-disgust and the ever-present heart-pounding fear. But if he threw up, he knew exactly what Ace would have to do.

He had to be tough. Tough enough to survive. Tough enough so that Ace would leave him alone and torture someone else. Anyone else.

It was his own fault. If he could make more mistakes, be more of a disappointment, Ace wouldn't try to mold him, make him. If he could be less, this wouldn't happen.

Sometimes he even believed that, no matter that it was a sad, self-serving lie.

You are not a child.

But he felt it. Felt those old feelings and thoughts taking over as if they were a spirit set on possessing him. He couldn't get the words out of his head, the pleas he'd offered as a child desperate for the pain to stop.

"So much potential in you, Gage. And you failed all of it. What you could have been. What you could have done. You've failed. Just like Jamison and Cody. Did you know they could have killed me? Both of them. It'd all be over. Instead, here I am."

"Do you want to see if I'll kill you?" Gage asked, giving the bonds that held him a little jerk. "I'd be happy to oblige that little experiment."

Ace laughed. "We'll get to it. We will. I'll give you all a chance to end me, because only the one who ends me could ever take my spot."

"We don't want your spot."

"One of you will. I was chosen for a reason, Gage, and one of you will be, too. Perhaps you six are my great challenge. My cross to bear. Every leader faces them."

"I can't decide if you're crazy or just evil, but *you* barely run your own gang anymore. You're hardly a leader. Seems to me, the Sons don't need you, Ace. Hasn't jail taught you that?"

The next hit was so quick and vicious Gage howled in pain and shock. Ace's grin widened.

"The pain can end. You know how it can end."

"I'm not worried about your pa—" Another crack and painful slap, though this one wasn't as hard or unexpected. Gage breathed through it, even as he felt blood begin to trickle down his thigh inside his pants.

Based on his father's reaction, Gage knew one thing. The Sons *were* struggling without Ace at the helm. Ever since Jamison and Cody had managed to get Ace behind bars, the Sons had been sloppy.

Or maybe…

Could it be that the *Sons* weren't struggling at all. It was Ace, losing power over the group that had followed him blindly. Wouldn't that be worse to Ace— continuing on just fine without him and so many of his top men dead after a planned explosion by Cody's former North Star Group?

The thought—the utter possibility—almost made

Gage laugh. It reminded him that *everything* had an end. And maybe he wouldn't live out his father's end, but his brothers would.

Felicity would.

She wasn't here, and neither was Michael. There were too many scenarios, too many possibilities of where Felicity could be and what she could be facing.

He had to survive this next little while just to make sure she survived. To make sure.

Then he did the thing he'd sworn to never do again.

Because sometimes you had to break a promise to yourself to keep a more important one to someone else.

"I get the whip because I'm the biggest. The smartest. The one best suited to take over, but the weakness of my mother needs to be beaten out of me."

Another blow, but he'd been expecting that, too. Giving in to what Ace wanted never truly offered relief. If it were that easy, life would be a heck of a lot different. For all of them.

"Isn't that how it goes?" Gage asked, failing to make his voice sound properly deferential.

"Try again. Try to mean it this time. Feel the truth. The weakness will be whipped out of you, Gage. Here. Or you'll die. Jamison won't save you this time. Brady won't save you. Even that little redheaded dimwit can't save you. It's you and me."

"And one of us will end up dead."

"Oh, son, now you're speaking my language."

Chapter Thirteen

Felicity may have lived with her father only until she was four years old, but as she waited to take him out, she realized she'd learned quite a few things from him.

Silence was the first thing. Stillness the second. If you were silent and still, it was hard to become a target. And in a house with her father, she was always a target.

He had to find her first, though.

She'd learned to fold in on herself, to meld into her surroundings with everything she had. She'd learned and honed those skills before she'd learned how to speak or walk—or so she thought. So she *felt*.

Life with the Knights, and the slow—very slow—bloom of maturity and adulthood had helped her unlearn those impulses. She'd figured out how to speak and move and dream and believe without folding in on herself. Without hiding.

But a person never unlearned their early impulses completely. As her father huffed and puffed toward her, she struggled to stay in the present. Hard when she was hiding just as if she'd been that toddler struggling to hide from another one of her father's rages.

But she had a plan this time. She had fight this time. Her father didn't get to terrorize her anymore.

She moved with his movements, keeping her body shielded by the large rock she was hiding behind. She was careful of where and how she stepped—even a pebble tumbling down the side of the crevasse she was tiptoeing around might bring his attention to her.

Though, based on all his heavy breathing, maybe not.

She kept her breathing even, that old hiding trick in full force as he passed the rock she was behind—as she moved around it so she could surprise him from the back.

She didn't even need to push him. As she jumped out, guttural scream piercing the quiet air, he jerked, tripped and tumbled down the steep cliff.

He landed with a thud, and then moans of pain that echoed and grew louder and louder. He writhed on the hard ground below and Felicity looked down at him. She felt inexplicably *furious*.

She'd won, for the moment. Done exactly what she planned to do, and still the fury swept through her like a tidal wave.

"Do you feel big and powerful now?" she called as she considering kicking some rock down on top of him. Or maybe throwing the heaviest rocks she could lift. She wanted to torture him. She wanted to cause him all the pain he'd caused her. She wanted to…

She stopped herself, and the fury. She wasn't like him—didn't want to be. She didn't need to terrorize him just because he'd terrorized her. It wouldn't solve anything or erase anything.

Still, it surprised her how badly she wanted to.

"Felicity." He said it in the same tone of voice she remembered. Pleading. Apologetic. Therapy had taught her that an abuser's strongest weapon was his ability to make himself seem truly sorry, truly sympathetic.

"Maybe you should answer the question. Do you feel big and powerful now?"

"I was only following orders, Liss. That's all. Ace is a powerful man. I had to do what he said. Please. Don't… I'm sorry. I had to."

He was a big lump on the ground, holding on to his leg. She stood quite a few feet above him. He was begging and pleading, and it was only the therapy she'd had that kept her from falling for it.

"You didn't *have* to do anything. Ace doesn't own you. You weren't…" Then it dawned on her, what she'd never fully considered. "You're *in* the Sons?" He had been. All this time. Somehow? Or was it new?

Did it matter?

No. What mattered was he'd killed his daughter— a sister she'd never known—and then tried to frame Felicity for murder. Regardless of Ace's influence, he had done those things. She was sure of it.

"You *killed* her," Felicity said, her voice vibrating with an emotion she wished she could bury for right now.

"Killed who?" His eyes bulged in horror down there in the canyon. "I ain't killed *no one*."

She believed him, for a split, stupid second when

she felt a moment of relief and hope. She desperately wanted to believe her father wasn't capable of murdering his own daughter, despite all the evidence to the contrary.

But that was so utterly ignorant she hated herself for even thinking it, no matter how briefly.

"Is Ace telling people I killed somebody?" He scrambled to stand and howled in pain. Presumably he'd seriously injured his leg. "I didn't kill nobody!" he shouted, panic and desperation tinging his words.

"And yet your fingerprints were all over my cabin. *And* the evidence. You're the one who identified her body."

"I didn't! I didn't! Whose body? What are you talking about?"

Felicity faltered. Michael seemed utterly confused and lost, and it wasn't beyond Ace, even in prison, to be able to make things happen. But how could someone have impersonated her father to identify a body? How could prints be dropped without her father being culpable?

"What about your daughter?"

"You're my daughter, Felicity." He managed to get to his feet, leaning on one leg over the other. He put his hands together as if praying. To her. "Please. You gotta help me. Ace made me do all this, but I didn't kill anyone. Please."

"You beat me. I was three years old, probably younger when it started. You beat me. A little, defenseless girl."

He had the decency to drop his arms to his sides. He

made a helpless gesture. "I… Yes, I did that. I know it makes me a monster. I was messed up. I still am. I get it." He didn't make the pleading motion again, but he did look up imploringly, shading his eyes against the sun with his hand. "But I didn't commit *murder*."

Maybe he hadn't. Maybe he had. She didn't know. She wasn't sure she cared.

"You deserve what you get," she said, but it was a whisper and she knew he didn't hear her down there. "You deserve what you get," she repeated, still whispering, feeling tears sting her eyes.

But it seemed more than possible that her father was just a pawn in Ace's scheme. Not an innocent one. He was in the Sons, had to be, whether he'd always been or had joined up recently. He deserved anything he got— and more than that, he didn't deserve even a second of her concern or help.

"I didn't kill anyone," he said, his voice wavering as if he was about to cry.

"Maybe," she agreed, feeling detached. As though she was floating above herself or as if there was cotton shoved into her chest instead of a heart and lungs. "It doesn't matter."

She could hear the way she sounded. Flat. Emotionless. There were emotions—she could feel them swimming under all that cotton—but she was afraid of what would happen, what she would allow herself to do if she accessed them.

She stepped back from the ledge.

"Felicity. Where are you going? You can't leave me down here!"

She took another step.

"Please! Please. I'm hurt. Don't… I'll die down here. I'm *hurt*. Please. Please!"

"I remember begging," she said. The sun was beating down on her, but all she felt was ice. Brittle, stinging ice. She had to get away from it.

Away from him.

"You'll probably die down there."

"Then it'll be you committing murder, Felicity," he yelled from his spot down in the canyon as she walked away.

"So be it," she whispered to herself.

GAGE WEAVED IN and out of the pain, out of consciousness. The blows kept coming, and would, until his father was ready to fight.

Usually at the point Gage was his weakest. But when a boy was at his weakest, that's when he fought the hardest. Or should.

According to Ace.

He'd be brought to his weakest point, then be given a weapon. A smaller, less useful weapon than his father's, but a weapon nonetheless.

Gage had survived this a few too many times to count. His own personal hell. His punishment for having a quick mind. For being born big and strong.

Gage was under no illusion he was special. Ace had picked on them all for separate reasons. Doled out punishments specific to each of his sons.

Gage had never told his brothers the whys of his

personal hell. Instead, he'd worked to make himself the opposite of everything Ace said he was.

Once he'd finally got into school, he'd failed. Over and over again. He'd skimmed through graduation from high school to the police academy. He never let himself excel, and since Brady did, and so well, no one ever thought twice of the underperforming twin.

Thank God. A saving grace.

Now he was back here, in the exact position he'd escaped, the exact position he'd proved to everyone he didn't belong to be.

He couldn't think about being back in this same place he'd escaped. Couldn't think about how unfair it was.

Maybe Ace was right all along. He was anointed somehow. Chosen. Because somehow Ace always got what he wanted, even if it took years to get there.

No. No, it wasn't true. Jamison was alive and well, getting ready to marry Liza and make a family with Liza's half sister. Cody was back with Nina and their daughter Brianna, building a life in Bonesteel.

Ace didn't get everything he wanted.

Gage fought off the nausea, reminded himself not to float away from the pain because that would only prolong the inevitable.

This standoff was inevitable.

Always had been. Always would be.

And if he ended it, maybe he'd be like Ace, but maybe he'd end this for his brothers. Would that be so bad? So wrong? Couldn't he live with anything if it meant saving his brothers?

"I think you're ready, Gage."

Gage laughed. It was all so ridiculous. He'd been whipped and beaten bloody—he could feel the blood covering him. Like a film.

This was Ace's language, Ace's currency. Blood and pain.

It could be Gage's, too. If he killed Ace, by some grace of God, it would be his language, too.

He didn't want it. He'd rather die. If he just knew Felicity was safe, he'd rather die. But he wasn't sure. He had to fight to be sure.

He was tired of fighting the insanity of his own father. Tired of fighting, period. He just wanted…life. He'd taken for granted the years since his escape when Ace had left him alone thinking they'd just keep lasting.

Gage looked at the man who'd fathered him, tortured him then and now, and had no doubt murdered Gage's mother. Gage didn't understand any of it. Top to bottom. "Why didn't you just kill us, Ace? You had the chance. Over and over and over. You've always had the chance."

Ace stepped closer, looking at Gage as if he'd missed some important life lesson along the way. "What's life without the chance? You've made me into a monster in your own head, Gage. You all did. None of you ever tried to understand. I don't want you dead. I want you reborn as only mine."

Reborn. It was such insanity. As if his own mother could be erased from him even if he wanted her to be. After all, she'd been weak enough to love a monster, to keep giving birth to son after son this monster would torture. Just to stay alive. And for what? To die anyway.

In the moment, he had no warm feelings for the mother who'd allowed this, but she hadn't been a monster. She hadn't been *this*. "She was better than you, you know," Gage said, expecting the blow to follow.

It didn't. Not yet. Ace got very still. "She was weak. And so are you."

"It isn't weak to survive you, Ace."

"She didn't, did she?"

"She did. She knew who and what you were. She couldn't break free of the spell of that, but she knew. She used to tell all of us that when she died, that when *you* killed her, you would try to make us into you. She said we never had to turn into that, if we didn't want to. She was stronger than you where it counted. We didn't escape until she was gone. Why not, Ace?"

"You really want to play the why-not game?" Ace smiled, the chaotic, gleaming smile that made Gage's stomach roil completely separately from the concussion symptoms.

If Ace was talking, though, he wasn't whipping or beating, so Gage nodded. "Yeah, let's play."

"Why didn't your mother escape? Why didn't she run you all to your precious grandma? She could have."

"Of course. She wasn't a prisoner to you *at all*," Gage said, letting the words drip with sarcasm.

"You six escaped. Why couldn't she?"

Gage opened his mouth to rage about how Ace had

warped his mother, twisted her until she didn't know *how* to escape. Maybe that made her weak, but she'd given Gage himself the belief that something better existed out there. He just had to get there.

Maybe it was Jamison who had proved it, over and over again, but it was his mother's seed of truth that he'd first believed.

But he was tired. God, he was tired. And his mother was dead. What did this matter? What did any of it matter? Why couldn't he give up?

He, of course, knew the answer. Felicity was out there, and as much as his brothers would survive and thrive without him, they would blame themselves. They would want to avenge him.

"Maybe she didn't want to bring your insanity to her own mother's household."

Ace snorted. "Your mother thought as little of Pauline as I do."

"And yet Pauline lives. Thrives. She raised us. And you let her. Why is that?"

Ace's face went dark, the terrifying fury Gage had once known better than to poke at. But he couldn't hold himself back, not when his own fury was beginning to bubble under all the pain and exhaustion.

He smiled at Ace in that same way Ace was always smiling at him. "You're afraid she really did curse you." Gage laughed. "That's just sad."

A blade flicked out—Gage didn't know from where—but it was at his throat, sharp and deadly.

"I was wrong, Gage. Rare, but we all make mistakes. Even me. I thought you were the smartest. But you're the weakest, and now you'll die. Say your last words, son. Because I'm done trying to make you into something."

Chapter Fourteen

Felicity licked her lips even knowing it wouldn't help the dry, cracked texture. It wouldn't magically make water appear or make everything swirling around in her mind make sense.

She was close to her cabin. Close to water. That was all that mattered as the sun beat down on her from above.

She squinted against the sun and stopped in her tracks when she saw what sat outside her cabin in the distance.

A police cruiser.

For a moment she felt relief so potent tears stung her eyes. She started forward, then remembered she was still wanted for murder.

Even if the police had saved Gage, that didn't mean things had been cleared up.

But they could be. Wasn't water more important than getting arrested? Gage would clear it up and everything would be fine.

Eventually.

Maybe.

I didn't kill anyone.

Her father had seemed so desperate. So surprised. So confused by what little she'd said about the murder. Was it her own bias doubting he'd killed, or was it just reason? *I didn't kill anyone. I didn't kill anyone.*

Ace had to have framed him, but how could she prove Ace was behind anything when he'd been in jail? And why would she want to? Her father deserved whatever he got.

Dying of exposure?

She pushed that thought out of her head, but the roiling nausea that accompanied it stuck around.

She slowed her pace as she moved toward her cabin. There was no sign of Ace or Gage. She used as much cover as she could to creep closer and closer to the small grove of trees that had been planted on the east side to give the cabin some shade back in the days before air-conditioning.

She hid among the trees, straining to hear something that might give her an idea of why the police were here. Had they found Gage? Ace? Was everyone okay?

Or was it all much worse than that?

The vehicle was a Pennington County cruiser, so there was no chance it was one of the Wyatt brothers, who all worked for Valiant County.

She didn't realize two men were in the cruiser until the driver's side door opened, and the passenger side next.

Two men got out. They clearly weren't in any hurry. Had they just driven up before she'd crested the rise for the cabin to come into view? That would mean Ace had taken Gage somewhere before the police had shown up.

She closed her eyes against the pounding panic. She had to figure out what was going on.

"Doesn't look like the tornado disturbed much here," the taller officer said to the other as they moved slowly toward the cabin. Not out of fear, but as if they weren't in any hurry to get to work.

"Lucky for us."

"Going over the house again seems overkill, doesn't it?"

The shorter one scratched his head. "That detective from Valiant County was adamant. Hard to blame him. Seems off if it's true the suspect didn't have any contact with her father."

"Seems *convenient* more than *off*, given he's friends with the suspect." The officer stopped short and swore. "Someone's been here. The tape's off."

"Could have been the wind," the other one said, but he was already pulling on rubber gloves and reaching for the caution tape fluttering in the slight breeze.

Tucker was the detective from Valiant County they were referring to. It seemed they were here only to search her cabin again. Look for more clues.

What might they find?

Didn't matter. She had to find Gage. There was no indication they had any idea he'd been here, or that Ace had.

Before she went in search of Gage, she needed backup. She had to forget about the desperate need for water and connect to the Wi-Fi.

But she'd need to be closer than the trees. Somehow, without getting caught. She could wait them out, but how long would that be? How long could Gage survive whatever and wherever Ace had presumably taken him?

Maybe he'd fought Ace off. Maybe…

Well, she couldn't entertain maybes until she knew for sure. She had to get a message to the Wyatts, then figure out what happened.

Without getting caught.

She closed her eyes for a second, letting herself pray to anything and everything she believed in, then she grabbed her phone. She pulled up the Wi-Fi and watched the screen as she crept closer and closer.

"Come on," she muttered, waiting for her Wi-Fi name to come up. She was easing out of the trees, her gaze moving from the cabin to the phone, back and forth, back and forth.

"Someone was definitely in there."

Felicity jumped back, pressing herself behind a tree. She squeezed her eyes shut and held her breath. She couldn't hear over the pounding of her own heart in her ears. She was light-headed and afraid for a moment she might faint.

Then the engine started.

She dared peek from behind the tree and watched as the police cruiser drove away.

She nearly wept in relief. Still, she waited, making sure they were gone for good before she ran forward. She had to stop, drop her pack and dig for her keys.

With trembling hands, she found them and ducked under the caution tape.

It took a while for her hands to stop shaking enough to insert the key into the lock. She pushed it open and went straight for the faucet. She flipped on the water, ducked her head under the stream and drank with messy, greedy gulps.

Once she cooled off a little bit she remembered herself and her priorities.

She pulled up the text messages on her phone and sent a group text to everyone—Wyatts, Knights.

Ace was at my cabin. Took Gage. Don't know where. Going to track. Need help.

She paused, stupidly, then took the time to explain where she'd left her father and that he'd need help and medical attention.

She couldn't be that cold to let revenge take over her.

He beat you. Gage's words, flat as they'd been when he'd first delivered them, echoed in her head.

She shook her head. What was done was done. She'd sent the text and now she had to find Gage.

She grabbed the few water bottles she had left and went back outside, locking the door behind her. She ducked back under the tape, pushed the water into her pack and studied her surroundings.

She could see a myriad of footprints. Had the cops even looked at them? She focused on them now, remembering this morning.

Ace had tossed her down, and there was the indentation in the grass where she'd slid. There was a boot print—presumably one of the cop's—in the middle of it.

She moved there, then turned to look at the house. Ace had held Gage, that horrible gun pressed to his temple, right there and—

Gun.

She bolted back into the house, knowing it would take too long and knowing she had to do it. She got her gun and holster, then returned to where Ace had held Gage.

She tried to determine whose footprints were whose, followed the two sets that veered off behind the house. One had to be Gage's, didn't it? If her father had followed her, his prints wouldn't be aligned with Ace's *or* Gage's.

There was mud here, not sloppy mud, but slowly drying mud. Still wet enough to make deep marks, but more of a clay texture. A flurry of footprints, a few indentations she couldn't figure out, but it all ended in a set of footprints and two long trenches.

Like heels being dragged. Fear snaked through her, but she couldn't give in to it.

She followed them.

They went for a way, into the patch of grass behind her cabin. Still, the ground was soft enough she could follow it.

Until the grass gave way to rock. The millennia of wind and rain, soil and rock. Erosion and deposition in its grand, epic scale.

Her heart, stretching out before her, and the absolute worst landscape she could encounter when trying to find someone. Rock was vast, virtually trackless. Too much wind to follow any kind of idea of which way they'd gone.

Then she saw it. A little bit of fabric under a rock. Black, like the T-shirt Gage had been wearing. Just a bit of it, clearly ripped off.

You're being unreasonable. If he was being dragged away, how could he rip his shirt *and* stick it under a rock?

Unless he was doing the dragging, but wouldn't he have gotten help? Not dragged Ace off alone?

It was probably just something blown by the wind— a hiker tearing his clothes on a rock, or the remnants of a ceremonial object. Granted, those occurred more often in the southern portion of the park. Still, with the winds in the Dakotas it was hardly impossible.

But this fabric was under a rock. Specifically. Purposefully.

If she went in the direction of the piece of fabric, she'd be heading back out into the canyons and rock formations.

That didn't scare her. She was a park ranger. She was equipped, now, with water. She knew how to navigate. She knew how to get back if she went in the wrong direction.

She glanced warily at the sky. She was prepared to camp. No food, but she had water. She had a weapon now. Everything would be fine.

Because she wouldn't stop until she found Gage.

She followed the bits of fabric, almost sobbed with

relief as she found a car insurance card with Gage's name on it. He had really been Hansel and Greteling it through the Badlands while Ace dragged him along.

How hurt was he, though, that he didn't fight off Ace?

She kept going, ignoring that thought as she followed the bits of Gage's things. She had to double back a few times when she couldn't find anything for a while. It was exhausting, and she should stop for water, but every time she found the next hint she pushed forward, desperate to find the next one.

She didn't touch them, hoping the Wyatt boys would be able to find them and him. If *she* could, *they* could, she was sure of it.

When she reached a clearing of sorts along a long wall of rock, she almost doubled back, but in the distance she saw something black and out of place against the tan, reddish and brown landscape.

She moved toward it, then stopped a few feet away.

It was a wallet. It sat in the open, which she thought was strange. It wasn't hiding. It wasn't under a rock— so technically the wind could have blown it.

Right above the wallet was the entrance to a cave.

Slowly Felicity lowered her pack to the ground, taking care to move quietly. She pulled the gun from the holster and crept toward the cave, her heart in her throat.

GAGE KEPT HIS gaze on his father as he waited for the pain. Would Ace slit his throat like he had the knife poised to do? Or would it be slower, meaner?

It could go either way, but for right now Ace simply held the knife there, waiting for Gage's last words.

He didn't have any. Not for his father anyway.

"Cat got your tongue? Maybe that's where I'll start."

Gage shrugged, even as he felt the blade of the knife scrape against the tender skin of his neck.

Ace paused, frowning. There was a noise, some kind of skittering like pebbles falling, toward the mouth of the cave. Likely some kind of animal, but Ace tilted his ear toward the sound.

Gage was weak, beaten, bloody, and still he knew a moment when he saw one. With enough of a push, he couldn't escape, but he could get that damn knife off his throat.

He used the bonds that held his hands tied behind his back and to whatever was behind him to hold his weight as he managed to slowly and quietly rear his leg back.

He made noise as he kicked, which was inevitable. Ace tried to sidestep the blow. Gage planned on that and managed to pivot with enough time for his kick to land, knocking Ace over, with some help from a rock formation behind him.

Ace snarled up at him. "You think you can win with your hands tied behind your back?" Ace demanded, a vicious, piping fury that overrode his usual distressing calm. *"You."* He got to his feet, searching the cave floor around them for his knife.

When he didn't see it, he began to reach for the gun at his side.

"He might not be able to. But I can."

Gage was sure he was hallucinating. The sun shone behind her like she was some kind of red-haired guardian angel, complete with firearm.

It wasn't possibly happening, but there Felicity was, stepping away from the streaming sunlight and into the dim light of the cave. She held her gun pointed at Ace.

She didn't shake. She didn't waver. She didn't look over at Gage himself. She just kept that gun pointed at Ace, her gaze cool and calm and locked on him.

Ace's sneer deepened. "You won't shoot me."

"I shot your man last month. Isn't that why you're after me now? Trying to pin a murder I didn't commit on me."

Ace laughed mirthlessly, and the sneer stayed put on his face. "Don't flatter yourself. You're a bug."

"A bug you can't squish." Her voice was so cool, so controlled, it very nearly sent a shudder through Gage. He wasn't sure he *knew* this Felicity. She was like a different person.

"Felicity—"

She shook her head, still not looking over at him. "I want you to loosen the holster, let it fall. Then you'll walk out of this cave, Ace. Hands up, walk slow. I'll follow. Then we'll all wait."

"You must have mistaken me for one of my sons. I'm not going to simper and follow along. You think that sad excuse for a gun scares me? *Me?* Do you know what I've survived? Do you know what I am?"

"I don't really care, Ace, because my finger is on the trigger and if you don't move in five seconds, you'll have a bullet to the gut."

"Let's see what you got, sweetie." He began to move for his gun—not to drop it, Gage was sure. "I'll be the nightmare you—"

The shot rang out and Ace's body jerked, stumbled, then fell.

Gage made some kind of noise—horror, shock, relief and a million other things wrapped up into whatever expulsion of sound escaped his mouth.

"Felicity."

She took a step back. She didn't seem so cool and calm now as Ace writhed on the floor. He held on to his stomach, blood trickling over his hands. She still had the gun pointed at him.

"Felicity," he repeated, trying to keep his voice calm. "Get the gun."

Ace was reaching for it, but every time his arm moved, he groaned or grunted in pain. Color and blood drained from him with equal speed.

Felicity moved forward and slid his gun out of his holster without much of a fight from Ace.

She stared down at him, both guns in her hands now.

"Felicity. Come untie me."

She didn't move. She stared down at Ace's body as if she was in a trance. Ace writhed, made awful noises, but he didn't attempt to fight Felicity. Her finger was still on the trigger, the gun still pointed at Ace.

Gage didn't know whether she planned to shoot him again, and he certainly didn't know whether he wanted her to or not, but the pale, lifeless look on her face was killing him.

"Felicity. Look at me."

Finally, she turned. A breath escaped her, shaky and pained. Then she sucked it in. She was pale, the color of death. Her eyes were glassy and her breath was coming in shallow puffs now.

He couldn't make his way to her and it cut him in two.

"I had to." She flicked a glance at Ace again.

"You did the right thing," Gage said, trying to draw her attention back to him. "Grab his knife. Then come untie me, okay? We'll figure it out. One step at a time."

She nodded too emphatically for him to feel any better about her mental state.

"Right over there. By that big rock."

"It's a sediment pile."

"Sure, sure." Hearing her using the technical term was some kind of relief. "Bring the knife here, okay?"

She nodded again, and this time actually moved for the knife. Gage glanced at Ace. He was still moving, writhing and groaning.

She'd shot him in the gut, just like she'd warned.

Felicity slid her gun into her holster, still holding Ace's in her hand. She picked up the knife, both her arms shaking now.

"Felicity. Untie me. Come on. Felicity?"

"Right." She approached him, all shaking limbs and too pale complexion. When she finally reached him, still holding the knife and gun in either hand, she met his gaze.

"God…you're… Gage." She inhaled shakily, tears filling her eyes.

"I'm okay. Kind of. I mean, I'll be okay. Look at me. I'm doing better than you, at the moment."

"You're covered in blood."

"It's okay. Don't cry, sweetheart. God, it's killing me. Just untie me. Okay. Untie me. I need you to untie me."

"I'm sorry. I'm sorry." She scrambled forward and began to work on the ropes with the knife. "My brain's in a fog. I can't seem to think."

"You're fine. You saved me. You're all right."

"Saved… I… Did I kill him?"

They looked over at Ace. He'd stopped writhing, but his eyes were open and full of hate. Directed at them.

"Get me untied, Felicity," Gage said flatly.

"I'm trying. I'm trying." She was practically chanting it, but he could *feel* her shaking behind him as she worked.

Gage kept his eyes on Ace. Ace didn't move. When he opened his mouth as if he was trying to speak, little more than a groan escaped.

All this time, Gage had dreamed of Ace's end, and he didn't know what to feel in the face of it actually happening.

When Felicity finally managed to cut and untie the bonds, Gage at least felt relief instead of uncertainty. He stumbled a little forward, shook the rope off, then turned to Felicity.

She was staring at Ace, anguish written all over her. She kept looking at Ace as she spoke. "I texted your brothers. I followed your trail, surely they'll be able to. But we should head back if we can. I don't know what to do about…" She trailed off, swallowed and then looked up at him. "You're so hurt."

He held her face in his hands and studied her eyes. Too unfocused. She was in shock and they had to get out of here. She shook underneath his palms as if she was falling apart.

He wouldn't let that happen. He pressed a kiss to her forehead. "Felicity. Hey, I'm here."

She inhaled sharply and let it out on something like a sob even though no tears fell onto her cheeks. "I left my father to die. I shot Ace. You're so hurt." She looked up at him imploringly. "I don't know what to do."

He wanted to scoop her up and carry her away, but he'd be lucky to walk out of this cave on his own. "We just gotta get out of here. You got a message to my brothers. They'll be here. Let's get out of this cave. You just need some fresh air. Come on." He let go of her face and winced at the blood he'd accidentally left there.

His body screamed in pain, but he couldn't let her see it. He took a step and tried to breathe through the shooting pain, but with the next step his leg buckled. He cursed and glared over at Ace, who'd made some gurgle of a sound. Almost a laugh.

He was smiling, but he wasn't moving. The color was draining out of his face and he just lay there, clutching the bleeding wound.

"You're going to die. A slow, painful death," Gage offered.

Ace's smile didn't die. It widened. "And won't that be funny?" Ace said, his voice a rasp. "This little girl with more strength of spirit than you worthless weaklings did what you couldn't."

Gage struggled to his feet with Felicity's help. She didn't speak as she helped him limp toward the cave opening. Gage refused to engage with his father.

Gage made it without falling again, though the opening of the cave required some climbing that had him trying to bite back groans. He wasn't successful, and by the time they were a few feet away from the cave, where he'd left his wallet, Felicity was crying, silently, the tears streaming down her face.

He couldn't stand any more, and he lowered himself to the ground in something more like a crash. She stumbled over to him, presumably to help him, but he just folded her into him.

She let out a sob, and then another, and Gage held her while she cried—while he kept an eye on the mouth of the cave.

He was pretty sure Ace was completely incapacitated, but he wouldn't put it past the man to magically heal himself and come out of that cave whole and ready to fight.

"We should head back," Felicity said, her voice a squeak.

"Not sure I can do that. Let's just wait."

"It's getting dark. They might not see the trail."

Gage held her close despite the pain ricocheting in his body. "They will. They will. Let's just rest up a bit." He felt like he was fading, but he held on to Felicity and she snuggled into him as they waited.

It didn't take too terribly long. The sun was beginning to set when he saw someone in the distance.

"There shouldn't be just one person," Felicity said, fear and concern lacing her tone. She got to her feet. "I only see one figure."

"They might have split up to track."

"I left my father, Gage. He was hurt. But it could be him. He said he didn't kill anyone. Didn't even seem to know about someone being dead."

"But Tuck said he ID'd the body."

"I know. I know. I don't understand any of this, and if Ace dies, we may never know."

"If Ace is dead, Felicity, everything will be okay. That I can promise you."

Chapter Fifteen

Brady reached them first, then was able to radio emergency services with directions. Though she protested, Felicity was whisked away to the hospital just like Ace and Gage.

She was discharged a lot quicker than they were, and then bustled away to the Knight Ranch, where Duke and Rachel and Sarah fluttered all over her before forcing her to go to bed.

Felicity hadn't slept. She tried. She closed her eyes, lay completely still and emptied her mind of *everything.* But in that numbness she couldn't find the release of sleep.

Still, she stayed in bed for a full eight hours. Awake. After that exercise in futility she was up and ready to just…do anything else.

Sarah was at her door before Felicity had even made it across the floor.

"You shouldn't be up."

"I stayed put eight hours," Felicity said, wincing at how much she sounded like a whining child.

Sarah's expression was disapproval, but she didn't push Felicity back to bed, so that was something.

"Is Gage home?"

Sarah nodded. "I just talked to Dev. They released him this morning. Brady took him home and Grandma Pauline's ordered him to bed. Tuck is staying at the hospital to make sure police are guarding Ace at all times."

"So…" Felicity had to say it, had to accept the strange dichotomy of feelings swirling inside of her. "Ace is alive."

Sarah nodded, a scowl on her face. "He went through surgery. The prognosis isn't great, but the longer he survives, the higher his chance of survival goes. Or so says Brady."

"I want to see Gage."

"Duke—"

"I'm going over there," Felicity said. She didn't know what it would do. She'd be fussed over there just as much as here, but…

She only knew what she had to do.

Sarah convinced her to take a shower first, and Felicity knew that while she was showering, Sarah was likely telling Duke what Felicity planned.

He'd want her to stay put, but she just couldn't.

When Felicity was out of the shower, dressed and ready to go, Sarah was waiting for her in the kitchen.

"I hope you're not missing chores for this."

"Chores can be made up. Besides, I'm just going to drive you over. Then I'll come back and do my work. Duke or I will pick you up later."

"You both know the doctor said I was fine."

Sarah pursed her lips as if considering what to say in response, an odd thing for outspoken Sarah. Eventually she just shook her head. "Come on."

They drove to the Reaves Ranch. Felicity insisted Sarah not walk her to the door. If it had been Rachel or Duke, insisting wouldn't matter, but Sarah understood something about a woman needing to do things on her own two feet. "Felicity?"

Felicity paused before she slipped out of the car. She looked at Sarah, who kept her head straight ahead and her shoulders hunched practically up to her shoulders. Which Felicity knew meant she was going to say something genuine and meaningful.

"I hope you know you don't have to go through this alone."

Since it made her want to cry, especially coming from Sarah, Felicity shook her head. "What I was going through is over," Felicity replied, and got out of the car.

It might have been the biggest lie she'd ever told, but it felt right to say it. She walked across the yard and stepped into Pauline's kitchen without knocking— Pauline considered knocking a grave offense among her friends.

"There's a girl," Pauline greeted, standing in her normal spot by the stove. "You're looking peaked yet."

Felicity forced a smile. "I'm all right. Where's Gage?"

"Upstairs," Brady answered from his seat at the table, a mug of coffee next to his elbow and his phone out in front of him. "Still asleep or should be."

"Can I go see him?"

"Let's give him some time yet," Grandma Pauline said, nudging Felicity into a chair. A plate loaded with a country breakfast appeared in front of her.

Felicity could hear the sounds of little girls playing in the living room, so Gigi and Brianna were here, which meant Liza and Nina were, too.

She stared at the plate, knowing she should eat it for Grandma Pauline's sake. But despite her internal coaxing, she couldn't seem to force herself into actually doing it.

The back door opened and Dev stepped in, stomping his boots on the mat. "Any news?" he asked.

Brady shook his head. "Not since the last."

"Why are they trying to save the SOB?" Dev groused. "Worthless waste of resources."

"Doctors take a vow to heal anybody," Brady lectured.

Felicity felt numb. She didn't know why. Everything she'd done was what she'd had to do. Leave her father to die. Shoot Ace. She'd had to do all those things, and if two monsters ended up dead, didn't that make her a hero?

But she didn't feel good. She didn't even feel terrible. She felt empty, and being here didn't help.

She just wanted to see Gage. Make sure he was all right. If she did that, maybe everything would click back into place somehow. Maybe she wouldn't feel as though she were walking through a cloud.

Dev sat down and ate his breakfast, and Brady poked around on his phone and drank his coffee.

No one tried to fill the silence with conversation.

The only sounds were the girls in the other room and Grandma Pauline cleaning up after breakfast.

After typing furiously on his phone, Brady set it down and cleared his throat. "Jamison and Cody are on their way back to rest up for a bit before heading out again."

"Did they find my father?" Felicity asked, even though she knew the answer. Why would they head back out if he'd been found?

"No. Not yet. A few agencies are still looking, though. And they'll keep at it."

"He should be where I left him." They'd told her they hadn't found him when she'd been at the hospital last night, but she'd hoped by morning things would change. Daylight would make finding him so much easier.

Maybe the numbness would go away once she knew what had happened to him. "I don't understand why he wouldn't be."

"It could be he tried to find a way out, a way to safety. There are a lot of possibilities, Felicity. You said your father didn't kill that woman."

"That's what he said." She had no reason to believe it, no reason not to. What did it matter? Obviously, Ace had set him up one way or another.

"We'll keep looking for him."

Felicity nodded, the knot in her stomach becoming tighter and heavier.

"If you're worried or don't feel safe, you can stay here. We can—"

"I'm not worried. There's no reason to worry." She

stood and pushed away from the table with too much force—everyone in the kitchen looked at her and it made her skin crawl with the feel of their stares and assessment. "I need to talk to Gage. That's okay, right?"

Brady's brow furrowed, but he nodded. "I'm sure it'll be fine."

Felicity didn't even wait for instructions. She didn't know which room Gage would be in, but she'd figure it out. Of course, as she stepped into the living room heading for the stairs, Liza and Nina stopped her.

Liza enveloped her in a hug almost immediately. "We're so glad you're okay." She pulled back and studied Felicity's face. "You need to sleep."

Felicity tried to muster a smile. She didn't bother to lie to Liza, who'd always seen through them all with a mother's knowledge. "I tried."

It had been hard to lose Liza when she'd gone back to the Sons to save her half sister. Hard to have her back, too. Felicity hadn't fully accepted Liza's return at first—she'd still felt a little hurt and betrayed. In the moment, she couldn't access any of that bitterness.

She was just glad someone could see through her. If someone could, maybe she'd make sense of herself, eventually.

"What's wrong with Aunt Felicity?" Brianna asked, forgetting her dolls with Gigi and coming to stand next to her mother. "Did Grandma Pauline make you some magic cocoa?"

Felicity managed a smile and slid a palm over the girl's flyaway blond hair. It was amazing how quickly and easily Brianna had slid into the family. Despite spending her first almost seven years away from Cody and the Wyatts, she'd had no problem accepting he was her father, accepting the crowd of aunts and uncles she now had.

It warmed Felicity some to remember what family and love could do. "No magic cocoa yet. I'm going to go check on Gage first."

"His head got smashed," Gigi said seriously.

"Not exactly," Liza replied on the long-suffering sigh of a frustrated parent. "The Wyatt boys need to learn to choose their words a little bit more wisely around small ears."

"Can we go up and see Uncle Gage?" Brianna asked. "I can give him my magic necklace."

"Uncle Gage has his own magic for now," Nina said. "We call them high-voltage painkillers that make him sleepy. You go on up, Felicity. I'm sure he'll be glad to see you."

Liza linked her arm with Felicity's. "I'll show you which room."

That tone, which meant *I'll drag all of your secrets out of you* had Felicity hesitating. "I can find the room. I—"

"Come on now," Liza said cheerfully, pulling Felicity toward the stairs.

Felicity had no choice. Liza pushed her in front to take the narrow staircase first, and she followed right behind.

"You know, Brady had to sedate him to keep him from charging over to the Knight Ranch and seeing you this morning."

For the first time in something like twelve hours, Felicity felt *something* pierce the numbness. Not much, but a little spread of warmth. "Oh."

"Oh."

"That's what I said. Oh."

"Felicity." Liza stopped her at the top of the stairs. "As someone who's been on the receiving end of a Wyatt man's concern, that was *not* friendly concern."

"What was it then?"

Liza narrowed her eyes and folded her arms across her chest. A very formidable *mom* look. "Care. Serious, love-type care."

"Love." Felicity's face got hot and the word came out like a croak. She didn't particularly want to feel embarrassment, but she supposed it was nice to feel anything. "You're being ridiculous."

"Am I?"

"Yes. He just kissed me is all."

"Is all." Liza took Felicity by the shoulders before she could continue down the hall. "But you've always liked Brady."

"I…" Felicity looked imploringly down the hallway. "I didn't even really *know* Brady, you know? It was just a safe crush."

"There is nothing safe about a Wyatt."

Liza laughed at the horrified look that must have crossed Felicity's face. Then she pulled Felicity into a hug.

"Babe, you *shot* Ace. There isn't anything safe about you, either. Revel in that a bit." She pulled her back.

"You saved Gage's life. But this one? It's still yours. Don't—"

"It isn't like that." Felicity didn't have the words, but she knew what she felt, what Liza was worried about. "It isn't like that. You know… How it feels like no one understands you? Deep down, I think all us foster sisters *could* have understood each other, but we were too self-absorbed to realize that. We weren't mature enough or something to access understanding, even when we had love."

Liza nodded sadly. "It's hard to see past your nose when you're that young, and that wounded."

Felicity nodded. It hurt she hadn't realized it before, but at least she understood it now. "He's the only person to make me recognize other people understand what I was feeling. To suck me out of feeling like I'm the only one who knows what certain things are like. To actually look and see all of me, not some half version. It's not transferring feelings or anything. It's… He just got me. And that matters. Does that make sense?"

Liza nodded, her eyes suspiciously shiny. "All the sense in the world."

GAGE STRUGGLED TO wake up. Something had changed. In the air. Inside of him. Something had changed, and he had to wake up to figure it out.

When he finally managed to blink his eyes open, the room swam. Back at the ranch. Last night at the hospital was a vague blur, but Brady had driven him home this morning, with strict orders to rest and heal.

It didn't sound so bad in the moment, his temples

pounding and his mouth dry as dust. His body ached everywhere. He was pretty sure his hair hurt.

Then a cool hand brushed his forehead, featherlight and soothing. He sighed into it a moment, half convinced it was some guardian angel.

But God knew he didn't have one of those.

He managed to move his head, and there was Felicity, sitting on the floor next to his bed. All he could see of her was her red hair, and the arm she'd put up on his bed to stroke his forehead.

"Am I about to have an illicit dream?"

She tilted her head up, giving him a skeptical if amused look. "I don't think so."

"Darn." He tried to move, but it all hurt too much. "What are you doing sitting on the floor? I can't see you down there."

She got to her feet, moving a few steps down the length of the bed so he could look up at her without having to crane his neck.

It hit him now, safe at home in his childhood bed, in a way it hadn't back in that cave. "You saved my life." He'd been prepared to die, if she was okay, but instead she'd stepped in and saved him.

It awed him straight through. Even if she didn't seem all that pleased.

She looked down at her hands. "People keep saying that. I don't remember much of it, to be honest. It just kind of happened." She shrugged helplessly.

She was too pale. She looked frail, like she had in that cave. Shaken and in shock, though she had a better grip on it now. She still wasn't…Felicity.

"Why don't you come sit down?"

She didn't. She just stood there, staring at him as if figuring out some great mystery. "Liza said you wanted to come see me. She said you had to be sedated."

He tried to shift in the bed, but just ended up wincing in pain. "Liza exaggerates. God, you smell good. Come here." He patted the bed next to him.

She studied the small spot, lips pursed, then carefully eased a hip next to him on the bed.

"If you wanted to, you know, caress my forehead again, weep a little over my wounds, I wouldn't be opposed."

He managed to get a snort out of her. Not quite a laugh, but an improvement to the seriousness. And even better, she drifted her fingers across his forehead.

They stayed like that for a few minutes, her moving her fingers back and forth on his forehead, a kind of balm even painkillers didn't offer.

And since it was making him relax, and he was too tired, too hurt to fight it, he reached up for a handful of her T-shirt and pulled her down until they were nose to nose. Then he kissed her, with all that softness.

She kissed him back, and something in her shifted or relaxed. Lightened, like a weight lifted. At least it seemed to him.

She pulled back a fraction, green eyes studying him with a kind of meaningfulness that might have sent him running far away if he could. But he couldn't. He was pretty much stuck here, and she made him feel...

She made him feel. Which meant it was time for a

joke. "Still like it without all the mortal danger clouding your judgment?"

Her mouth curved, and she didn't back away. "Yeah, it's okay."

"What's wrong, Red?"

She exhaled shakily. "I don't know. They can't find my father."

"If Ace put him up to everything, that's not so bad, is it?"

"I guess." She swallowed, searching his face as if the answers she needed were somewhere in him. "He could be dead out there. Because of me."

"You could have been dead a long time ago because of him. No matter what he did or didn't do in *this* moment. What happened to him, he brought upon himself."

She sat so still, didn't suck in a breath or let one out. It was as if she froze completely. But after a moment or so of that incomprehensible reaction, she gave a small nod. "You should rest," she said, easing away.

"You're looking a bit like you could use some yourself."

"I tried." She lifted her shoulders, then dropped them. "I can't."

He pulled her close and tugged the covers up around them both. "Give it a shot."

And they both slept.

Chapter Sixteen

As the next few days passed, everything was a bustle of activity.

Ace was going back to jail, more charges heaped on him. It would be harder and harder for him to hurt people on the outside. Though she knew no one fully believed he was powerless in jail, it was still safer having him there than in the hospital. And she knew the Wyatts were hoping the attempted murder charges would get him transferred to a federal prison.

She hoped so, too, but while they waited for the bureaucratic tape to be cleared up, Gage was healing. All the Wyatts were still insisting he stay out at the ranch instead of his apartment in town, but everyone knew he wouldn't acquiesce that much longer, nor would he need to.

The police had canceled the warrant for Felicity's arrest, which had been a relief on every level. And, best of all, she'd been cleared to go back to work starting Monday.

Added to that back-to-normal, she seemed to have come out on the other side of this whole ordeal with something almost like a boyfriend, though she hesitated to say that word aloud, especially since they hadn't exactly told anyone about them.

Still, while she stayed at the Knight Ranch and Gage healed at the Reaves Ranch and everything cleared up, they took walks, exchanged kisses and had gone for a picnic lunch yesterday.

The Wyatts treated her like some kind of conquering hero, and somehow shooting Ace, even if she hadn't killed him, seemed to get it through everyone's head that she was not still the shy, stuttering Felicity.

Everything was fine and good. Better than it had been before this whole nightmare started.

Except that her father was missing. And while there was an APB out for him, and he was considered a missing person *and* a person of interest in a murder investigation, there was no trace of Michael Harrison. Even with Jamison and Cody and even Brady spending time searching for him.

It was like being stuck in limbo. Had she killed her father, no matter how inadvertently? Or was he still out there? And would that make him dangerous?

Felicity had no answers, and no one else seemed too concerned about it, so Felicity could only pretend that life was good.

She seemed to be fooling everyone—even Liza— that she was happy as a clam. With Ace out of the hospital and back in jail as of this morning, the Wyatts were darn near jovial. So much so that they were having a big family dinner, complete with the Knights.

It was raucous and good. Felicity had hoped the

large group of people in Grandma Pauline's kitchen would make her feel better. Instead, the noise and cheer was just making her feel more like she'd lost her mind somewhere in that cave.

She forced herself to smile, even forced herself to eat, though her stomach roiled and cramped at the idea.

She didn't know why she couldn't let it go. Why she couldn't have some well-deserved celebration like everyone else in the room.

Except, their father was in jail. Hers was mysteriously missing.

He had to be alive or they would have found him. Why would he be alive and hiding? Was it because he thought he'd be blamed for the murder? Was it because he'd lied to her and he *had* murdered someone—his own daughter at that?

Felicity's head pounded with all the what-ifs and emotions they stirred up. When Grandma Pauline brought out dessert, Felicity excused herself, pretending she needed to use the bathroom.

She headed away from the dining room, bypassed the bathroom, and went toward the rarely used front door, instead. There was a rickety old porch swing out there. It didn't get much use, but sometimes Grandma Pauline did her mending there when she didn't have enough people to cook for.

Felicity lowered herself onto it. She needed to get it together, but she didn't know how.

She should be happy. She should be ecstatic. Maybe concern was normal, but…

It was just that she knew the Badlands. She knew

what it would have taken to survive, if hurt. He hadn't even been able to stand when she'd left him there.

Left him to die.

Somehow Ace was alive and her father, who probably hadn't killed that woman—her sister—was dead because of her.

Maybe the woman wasn't even her sister. Her father had said he hadn't identified any body. Tucker had looked into that, interviewing the morgue employees. None had been able to confirm or deny that Michael had been the one to identify the body. Might have been, or it might have been someone pretending to be him.

Felicity closed her eyes and let herself rock on the swing. She heard the dogs clatter up onto the porch and she leaned forward to pet them, trying to find some comfort there.

Something had to change. She couldn't go on pretending. Eventually she'd just explode.

But her feelings didn't seem to want to listen to her rational thoughts, and she simply felt stuck in this awful place of…

Guilt.

She turned her head toward the door when she heard it creep open, forced all her heavy thoughts away as Gage stepped out onto the porch.

He didn't seem surprised to see her there, or even confused. "Got room on that swing?"

Felicity managed her fake smile. "Of course."

Gage slid into the seat next to her, draped his arm around her shoulders and gave her a little squeeze. He petted one of the dogs that put its head on Gage's thigh.

"That smile's getting a little rough around the edges, Red. You might want to just let it go."

Somehow he made it easy to do. The smile died and she let herself lean into him. She didn't know how to explain what was going on inside of her, but he didn't seem to need her to.

"I know you're worried your father's still out there."

She wrinkled her nose. Okay, he didn't need to see through her *that* easily. "It's fine."

"If it was fine you'd be inside or enjoying even half of this shindig. Do you think he's going to come after you or something?"

Wouldn't that make things easy? Well, maybe not easy, but different. It made more sense than guilt. "Maybe."

"Ah."

She tilted her head up to look at him. "Ah what?"

"It isn't that they haven't found him, and that he may be alive. It's that he might be dead. And you'd have to blame yourself."

She blinked at him, then looked out at the late summer sunset. "Neither are particularly positive potential outcomes, Gage."

"No," he agreed. "But I'm having trouble wrapping my brain around how you're feeling guilty for doing what you had to do to someone who made your childhood a living hell. Who could have made it a lot worse if the state hadn't stepped in."

She was supposed to blame him for that. And maybe he would have been bad enough to kill her back then. She only had hazy memories of living with him. She'd done her best to push them away when she'd been younger, and now they were hard to access.

She could remember pain. Hiding. Fear and confusion, but it was hard to attribute it to a specific face. All those reactions and impulses had come back easily enough when he'd been after her, but it still hadn't been the same.

The monster from her childhood was a faceless one. The man she'd left to die had been flesh and blood. She knew that didn't make sense, that it wasn't *right*, but it was all inside of her anyway.

She inhaled and let the breath out just like her therapist had taught her. "I—I don't like the i-idea I used the Badlands against him." The deep breathing didn't take away the stutter in the moment, but she'd gotten her feelings off her chest.

"Oh, Felicity," he said on a chuckle as he leaned his temple on the top of her head. "Leave it to you."

She slumped in the seat, but his arms stayed tight around her. "It sounds stupid," she muttered.

"No, it sounds like you. And I get it. It isn't like I don't understand. I can stand over here and think you shouldn't feel guilty that you might have left your father to the fate of the Badlands, since I know what he did to you. But I didn't experience what he did to you. Hell, everything we had with Ace is fifty kinds of warped. I wanted him to die, but I'm not sure it would have been any kind of relief if he did."

It was strange to have someone give words to feelings she didn't know how to articulate, but that's just what Gage did. When he did, it helped her find her own words. "I hate feeling this way, but I don't know how to make it stop. Not until I know for sure. Everyone expects me to be happy, and I just—"

"Sweetheart, you don't have to pretend to be happy just because everyone expects you to be. And let's be clear, Dev never expects anyone to be happy."

She managed a true smile at that. "I should be happy."

"If you're not, you should take your time to get right inside." He squeezed her shoulders again. "Give yourself a few breaks. We clawed our way through a rough few days there—it's okay if you're not ready to jump right back into normal life."

"You are *not* my normal life." This, him... She liked it, more than liked. But it didn't feel like her life to have a hot guy want to spend time with her, to slip his arm around her, to kiss her brainless.

"I am now," he said firmly.

It didn't *fix* her problems, but that determined sincerity eased some of the tightness. She'd still have to deal with whatever had happened with her father once they found him, but she'd have someone who understood the complexity of emotions over it...right next to her.

She tilted her head up. "You sound pretty sure about that."

He tapped her chin. "I am."

It was nice. Something and someone to be sure about, so she pressed her lips to his. He kissed her back, but he let her lead. He seemed to know the difference—when she wanted to be swept away, when she needed to be in control of something.

More than that, she understood the same about him. When he was content to sit back, and when he needed to push forward on something.

She sank into that kiss. Pushing forward. She'd been sitting around sulking, basically, but that was over. She had to act. She had to grab her life—*her life*. Why did bad men get to rule her life?

Not anymore.

She pulled away a fraction. "Are you going back to your apartment tonight?"

"Um." He cleared his throat. "I wasn't planning on it."

"Maybe we should." She didn't give him a chance to answer. Instead, she pressed her mouth to his again. When he deepened the kiss, pulled her so close she could scarcely catch a breath, she figured that was a *yes*.

The door creaked open, and though Felicity jumped back, Gage kept his arms around her and gave a withering look to Brady, who was staring at them with bugged-out eyes and a wide-open mouth.

"Help you?" Gage prompted.

"Grandma Pauline told me to—um." Brady cleared his throat. "Well." He rocked back on his heels and shoved his hands in his pockets. He looked embarrassed, which was kind of funny.

Felicity couldn't remember Brady ever looking embarrassed or uncomfortable. She couldn't remember

ever seeing him with *any* elevated emotion, and it so-
lidified what she'd been finding with Gage.

Brady was, on the surface, easy and nice. But Gage
was… Real. To her. Likely Brady would find someone
to be real for, but it wasn't her.

"Grandma Pauline wants to shove us full of dessert," she supplied for him.

Brady did not look directly at them, still sitting on
the swing with their arms around each other. "Yeah."

"Ready, Red?" Gage asked, giving her hair a little tug.

She was ready. Ready to stop wallowing and won-
dering and actually do something. A few somethings,
in fact. She got to her feet. "You bet."

GAGE MOVED TO follow Felicity, but Brady stepped in
between them, allowing Felicity to move forward and
stopping Gage from following.

Gage couldn't say he expected the censure on his
brother's face, but seeing it now wasn't such a grand
surprise. Brady had a lot of internal rules—not just for
himself, but for everyone.

"Looks like I'm staying outside to talk to my twin
brother, darlin'. You go on inside."

Felicity gave him a disapproving look. "Don't do
that. You don't have to do that." She turned to Brady.
"And you don't have to do whatever it is you have it in
your head to do."

Brady's expression remained carefully blank. "If
you'll excuse us, Felicity."

She rolled her eyes, muttered something about Wyatt men and headed inside.

Gage matched Brady's pose—stuffing his hands in his pockets, rocking back on his heels. He gave a cursory glance at the dogs sitting between them, tails wagging. "Nice night," he offered blandly.

"What exactly are you doing here?"

"Well, Brady, as I've known you to do the same with a handful of pretty women, I'm going to let you spell that one out yourself."

"You shouldn't—"

Gage might have had patience for Brady's lectures if he wasn't grappling with something bigger, broader than he was particularly ready for. "She's not your responsibility. And she certainly doesn't need your protection. Not from me."

"No. She isn't and doesn't. She isn't your responsibility, either."

"And that means what exactly?"

"What *is* this?" Brady gestured helplessly. "Felicity?"

"Yes, Felicity." He didn't have doubts there. Maybe he had some doubts about himself, about how right or ready he was for what he felt, but his feelings were there. And Felicity was too important to allow himself or Brady or anyone to convince him he should run away from them.

"You can't *fool around* with one of the Knight girls. I never thought I'd have to tell you that. Duke only tolerates Cody at this point because he's Brianna's father, not because Duke *approves* of Nina and Cody. I don't think he has any reason to tolerate you fooling around with Felicity."

Gage was about to make a joke, even opened his mouth to do it. But Felicity had told him he didn't have to do *that*, and he'd known what she meant. Not to make a joke to diffuse tension. Not to be *Gage* about it, all things considered.

So, maybe instead of a joke he could just settle in with the truth, no matter how uncomfortable. This was his twin brother after all. They had survived the same things. Side by side. Two sides of the same coin. Sometimes it felt like they spoke a language no one else understood. He loved all his brothers with all that he was, but what he shared with Brady was something unique.

Surely, Brady's censure was concern. Just veiled in that very Brady disapproval. "Well, I guess it's a good thing I'm hardly *fooling around*," Gage ground out.

"What? You're in love with her or something?" Brady snorted, but it died halfway through as his jaw went slack. "Gage…"

"Look—"

"Felicity, of all damn people."

"What's it matter if it's Felicity?"

"You can be impulsive, and this is not the time to be impulsive." Brady jerked a thumb toward the door where Felicity had disappeared. "She's not the girl to be impulsive with."

Gage shook his head. He'd never felt sorry for Brady. Brady was the smartest, the most even-keeled of all six of them. Everyone liked Brady everywhere he went. He was the best of them.

If Brady didn't understand that love was impulsive and just plain inconvenient, but *there* and necessary and impossible to ignore, well, he did feel sorry for Brady and hoped his twin would learn someday what love—inconvenient, out-of-the-blue love—could do.

"She's not a girl, Brady."

"I know that."

"I don't think you get it. Even with everything she did—including save my life—I don't think you get it. That's okay. You don't need to. This is not a situation where we require your input."

Brady opened his mouth, but Gage shook his head. "Input. Not. Required."

"Fine," Brady replied tightly. "Then I guess we should get back to dessert." He turned for the door. "And Duke kicking your butt," he muttered under his breath.

Maybe. But it was a risk Gage would take—couldn't help taking. Still, with honesty came the need for more of it.

"Did he have a weapon—just for you?" Gage asked before Brady could go back inside.

Brady paused at the door. When he turned around it was slow and careful, his expression carefully blank. He didn't meet Gage's gaze when he spoke. "He threw knives. To teach me to expect the unexpected."

There was more to that, and Gage wanted to know it all, but they didn't have time to get that deep into it. "Did he tell you *you* were special, so he had to be harder on you?"

Brady let out a long breath, but when he spoke it was

detached and rote. "He said I was stupid and worthless, so he'd do what he could to make a man out of me."

Gage could only stare at his brother at first. He'd never imagined. Brady. By far the smartest of them, at least the one who tried the hardest. He could have gone to medical school and become a doctor if Grandma had had access to the money or the understanding of how college worked.

But it made a sick twisted sense, in that Ace way things clicked together. They were twins and Ace had somehow used that against them. Make Brady work harder. Make Gage shrink away from what he was.

Brady shrugged, an out-of-character, impatient gesture for him. "We don't talk about this. What's the point?"

"I would have said there wasn't one just last week, but now I think we should. All of us. It would make us stronger against him. When you can... When you can let it go and someone understands, it changes something, Brady. And we all understand."

Brady met his gaze then, something wry in his expression. "Yeah, maybe, but good luck getting through to Dev on that score."

"We'll work on it." Gage was certain they needed to. "And there's something else we need to work on. I want you to help me find Felicity's father. She can't rest until he's found one way or another."

"We're looking."

"I don't mean casually or leaving it up to Pennington County. I mean you and me. Really looking."

"You aren't up for it yet." Brady tapped his temple.

"That concussion was serious, Gage. The rest will heal no problem, but you don't want to take chances with your brain."

"Okay, so I'll take a few days. But…"

Brady sighed heavily. "She needs closure. And you're going to make sure she gets it."

"Damn straight." She'd saved his life. He loved her, as uncomfortable as he was with *that*. He owed her something. He'd give her this. Whatever it took.

Chapter Seventeen

By the time they managed to convince everyone that Gage was well enough to spend the night on his own, and that she would be fine going back to her cabin in the park alone—though neither precisely planned on being alone—Felicity was wound tighter than a drum.

But it was good to feel something—even anxiety and a weird giddiness. She walked outside with Gage, Grandma Pauline and Brady still in the kitchen grumbling about that fool boy and his hard head.

Most of her family had already headed back to the ranch, and she'd need to have Gage drop her off so she could get her car. She couldn't very well tell anyone Gage drove her back to her cabin. It wouldn't make sense.

"You're going to have to drive me over to my car. Otherwise, everyone is going to figure out where I went."

"I don't think we were fooling Brady any. He very clearly knows."

"So does Liza," Felicity murmured, tilting her head up and staring at the giant spread of stars above. Liza,

Jamison, Gigi, Cody, Nina and Brianna had all headed back to Bonesteel earlier, but Felicity had to wonder how long Liza would keep what Felicity had told her a few days ago to herself.

"So…" Gage took her hand in his as they walked to his truck.

She looked down at their joined hands, marveled at how quickly that just felt right. But with rightness meant she owed him the truth. "I'm not ready for Duke to know."

"Ah."

"It's just… All those years ago? Everything with Nina disappearing on the heels of losing Eva *and* Liza really messed him up, and we both know no matter how much he loves Brianna, he hasn't quite forgiven Cody for being part of the reason Nina stayed away with her so long. I don't want to hurt him." She owed Duke so much more than she'd ever be able to repay, and that seemed reinforced by seeing her biological father again.

"I don't think you being happy would hurt him, Felicity. Even if he shot daggers in my direction for a while."

"Maybe." Maybe Gage was right, but… "I need to do a few things on my own, *really* on my own, right now."

"You do understand that what you're suggesting by coming home with me is not something you do on your own?"

She swatted his arm, unable to contain the laugh. "Yes, I'm aware."

He took her by the shoulders, and rubbed his hands up and down her arms. "Are you sure you want to do this? Now."

She didn't hesitate, because Gage was the only thing that made sense right now. If she went after what made sense, then she'd find herself on even ground again. "Yes. I'm sure."

"Brady seems to think I'm being impulsive, and that I shouldn't be…with you."

"Well, it's a good thing Brady doesn't get a say." She saw some hesitation in him, and she knew it wasn't his own. It had been put there—that he should be careful, that she couldn't handle it.

She wouldn't let anyone push her back to that place where people thought she needed to be protected or handled with kid gloves just because she was shy or stuttered or had been abused as a child. No. "I know what I feel when you kiss me, Gage. And I know how much it means that you understand me. And I understand you. I think we both know how special that is."

He stared at her for a long time, then he nodded. "Yeah. Listen, I've got an idea. Trust me?"

She nodded.

"Get in the truck."

They both climbed into Gage's truck, and Felicity decided to relax, enjoy the nighttime drive over the short, rolling hills of the Reaves Ranch. She had a spiritual connection to the Badlands that existed for some unknown reason deep inside, but she'd been raised and loved on these rolling grasslands of the two ranches that had been her childhood. If the Badlands were her soul, the ranch lands southeast of there were her heart.

He drove out, deep into the heart of the ranch. All the way through the pasture, to the tree line that ran along what had once been a creek but rarely got a trickle these days. The Knight land was on the other side of the creek bed.

It was so distant people rarely came out here unless a cow was missing. He stopped between the old creek and the pasture fence. He turned off the ignition and made a broad gesture.

Felicity's eyes widened. "Outside?" She couldn't school the squeak out of her voice.

"Seems…right."

It did. She'd rather be out here than anywhere else, and it was coming to be that she wanted to be with him more than anyone else—even herself, a rare thought for an introvert like her.

He slid out of the truck and grabbed a blanket from the back seat, and she followed. The night was warm, though the breeze was cool. The world smelled like summer—grass and wild. And though it was very much night, sunshine lingered in the air.

He spread out the blanket, looking something like a ghost in the silvery moonlight. But he was no ghost. No apparition. He wasn't even a dream. Gage Wyatt was very real, and all hers.

Not what she'd planned, certainly. Not at all what she'd expected. And yet perfectly right, down to this. Understanding her enough to give her this.

The fog she'd been muddling through these past

few days was gone, and while she still had fears and concerns and complex emotions over what had transpired, this was simple. And true.

She rose to her toes and kissed him. The stars and moon shone, the breeze slid over them, and Gage kissed her until there was only him—her own universe for the having.

He laid her out on the blanket, covered her. There was no room for nerves—why would there be? Unlike everything else in her life, she was sure of this, sure of him.

Because he undressed her with reverence, whispered all sorts of wonderful things against her skin. He made her feel beautiful and whole and strong.

She'd always wanted to feel strong, and it wasn't that he was *giving* her strength—it was that he was showing her all the ways it already existed. And now that she saw, now that she knew, what couldn't she do?

She kissed him, touched him—tracing his bandages and the wounds Ace had marked on him with her fingers, with her mouth. She tried to imbue some sort of healing property to the touches, but when she opened herself to him, she knew what true healing was.

Acceptance. Understanding. Finding where you belonged. Building hope together.

She let herself surrender completely to pleasure and that hope, gave herself over to the wave of it. The immensity of it.

She'd been through too much for that to scare her—how much she felt, how much she wanted. There was no room for fear when he moved inside her, with her, together until a sparkling, all-encompassing pleasure pulsed through her.

He gathered her up close, wrapping them in the blanket, the stars vibrant and all but vibrating in their velvet South Dakota sky.

She snuggled into Gage, breathed the mix of him and outside. This had been the first step toward her future.

She knew what the next was, though she didn't want to think about it in the happy, sated afterglow.

Unfortunately, Gage wasn't going to like that one.

She'd ignore it for now, and she wouldn't tell him yet.

There were some things you had to do alone, no matter how nice it felt to be together.

GAGE HAD DRIVEN her back to her car so she could follow him to his apartment if only because she'd been fretful over his head wound.

He wasn't sure what sleeping out under the stars would do to make it worse, but he hated to see all that worry on her shoulders because of him. Even if he didn't mind a little fretting on her part, like she might feel some fraction of the care blooming inside of him.

Hell, it wasn't care, it was love. He kept wanting to deny it, but how could he when her red hair was spread out over his pillowcase? Her face was slack in sleep, one arm tucked under her pillow and one pressed up against his.

Felicity had spent the night in his bed, snuggled up

to him like she belonged there. It felt like she did. It felt like *she* thought it did.

Still there was a sheen of anxiety to it. Whether it was her missing father, the ever-present threat of Ace—no matter how many high-security prisons they put him into—or Gage's own nerves at the idea of loving someone so...

Perfect wasn't the right word. He'd be afraid to touch perfect, but she was perfect for him somehow. Matched.

He'd never thought he'd be in love—especially not with someone who'd been hung up on his brother not all that long ago. He'd never thought he'd find himself dreaming of a particular kind of future that wasn't: be a cop, have fun, protect his family from Ace.

He touched the bandage on his head. He was still achy and knew he wouldn't be cleared to work for a while yet. Maybe he could be doing desk hours by the end of the week, but Gage hardly looked forward to that.

So, he wouldn't look forward. He'd enjoy his present.

Felicity moved, yawning and stretching as she rolled into him. Her eyes blinked open, that dark, intoxicating green. Her mouth curved. "Morning," she murmured sleepily.

"Morning," he replied, his voice rusty—and not from sleep.

She pressed a kiss to one of the scratches on his arm. She didn't fuss over the marks Ace had put on him. Instead, she treated them with a kind of reverence that made him feel vulnerable, but not in that fearful way he had as a child. This was something else. Not weakness, not fear, but hope and love, he supposed.

"I need to get up and get going," she said, yawning again as her eyes seemed to focus and engage.

He had no doubt Felicity Harrison was a morning person.

"What's the rush?"

"I want to give my cabin a good clean, and I need to get my uniforms ready for tomorrow." She gave him a quick peck and slid out of bed. She grabbed her T-shirt from the floor and slid it over her head.

A pity.

She shook out her sleep-and-sex-rumpled hair and then began to separate it into sections. It was mesmerizing, but his brain kicked into gear over what she'd just said.

"Are you sure you should be out there all alone?"

She pushed out a breath and began to braid her hair. "No. But I think I have to. I can't live scared Ace might get through again and…" She paused twisting the band around the end of her braid and looked at him, a heartbreaking desolation in her gaze. "I haven't said this to anyone, but I don't think my father could have survived, Gage. I really think he has to be dead. Which means they might never find him. Not if animals got to him. It's so big, so vast, and I just have to live with the uncertainty I guess, but I'm mostly certain."

It killed him that she blamed herself, but he knew how sneaky and hard to shake blame could be. He got out of bed, didn't bother with his shirt and just pulled his boxers on. "Okay, but I want you to take one of those button things Cody makes. The emergency call. You shouldn't be out there without cell service. Regardless."

She frowned at him as he crossed to her. "I'll have my radio when I'm on duty."

"I'm talking when you're off duty, babe. It's a drive from here to there."

She wrinkled her nose and finished with her hair. "I do not like *babe*."

"Sweetheart, honey, darlin'." He tugged the tight braid. "Red."

Her mouth curved. "Red's okay."

And it was that, her standing there in a rumpled T-shirt, her hair smoothly braided and her smile still sleepy that did it, completely and irrevocably. "I love you, Felicity." He hadn't meant to say it out loud, or if he had, he hadn't thought it through. Things were different for her. He'd been halfway in love with her for something like two years, and she'd been mooning over his twin brother, no matter the reasons. "You should take some time with that. I've had longer to think about it."

She stared up at him as if she'd frozen when he'd said those words. She blinked once but, other than that, didn't move. But he knew she was thinking, taking it in, in that rational way of hers. "B-but l-love doesn't really have to do with thinking," she said thoughtfully, eyebrows knitting together. "Accepting it does, I guess, but love is there, either way."

"I don't know."

"You wouldn't have *chosen* to love me, Gage."

"Why not? You're beautiful and sweet and smart, and kind of a badass, if you haven't noticed."

She nearly grinned at that. "You're all of those things, too, you know." She inhaled deeply, keeping her gaze steady on his. Her hands curled around his forearms, and he was almost certain she was about to let him down gently.

"I love you, too," she said, instead. "Maybe I need to think some about what to do with that, but I feel it, either way."

He had to clear his throat to speak. "Well, same page then, Red."

She nodded, still staring up at him. "You know, when I got that first summer internship at the National Park Service, I didn't let myself really dream about someday getting the full-time position here at home. When I finally got it, I told myself I'd believe that my dreams could come true if I worked really hard."

"I think you ended up with the wrong twin," he half joked.

She shook her head. "No. Brady was a nice enough placeholder, but I didn't want *him*. I wanted someone kind and good who understood me and made me feel like…this. That was never him, not really. But it's been you."

"Well. Hell."

She grinned up at him, brushed a kiss over his mouth. "Come on, I'll make you some breakfast before I go."

He slid his arms around her waist, pulling her close, nuzzling into her hair. "I have some different ideas."

She leaned into him for a second, then gave him a little push. "I'm hungry." She laughed, sounding a bit bewildered, as if she couldn't quite believe this was all happening. "But maybe after."

Chapter Eighteen

It took a few days to work out, especially without any of the Wyatt boys being tipped off. They wouldn't let her do this thing, and she had to do it.

It required a secrecy she wasn't very good at, and then waiting for her own day off to align with when she could accomplish the task.

Getting back to work had been good. It kept her mind busy, and though she struggled to forget everything that had happened at her cabin or on the trails, it was better to struggle than to avoid.

Routines were good. Having a plan was better.

Now she was going to enact it. She felt sick and nervous leading up to it but it had to be done. When it was over, maybe she would tell Gage, even if it made him mad.

She couldn't tell him before. He'd stop her, and she would not be stopped on this.

Luckily, Gage was back at work, though he was relegated to desk duty until he had his checkup next week. He'd grumbled about it all morning. Felicity had let him grumble, made him breakfast, then sent him on his way.

It was a bit like… Well, she didn't like to think about it too deeply, but waking up with him, whether at his apartment or her cabin, felt a bit like living together.

She shook her head as she got out of her car. Thoughts for another time. Today wasn't about Gage or how good she felt there. It was about closing the book on the unfinished chapter that still weighed on her, even if Gage allowed her to take a considerable amount of that weight off at any given time.

She tried not to think too hard about Gage as she pulled into the jail parking lot. He would hate this. He wouldn't understand it, and he was going to be so ticked off when he found out.

He had no one to blame but himself, though. He'd been the one to tell her she didn't have to be happy just because everyone expected her to be. He'd been the one to help her find the courage to do this.

He'd hate that even more.

Now she was here, and she was ready. She'd close the door on this, if she could, and then her life wouldn't feel like it was in an awful limbo.

Felicity stepped into the jail, followed the instructions to be a visitor, and then was taken into a room with plexiglass partitions. She took a seat and waited. She breathed through her nerves and focused on portraying a calm, unflappable exterior.

It didn't matter if she was a riot of nerves inside. If Ace didn't see it, it wouldn't matter at all.

It didn't take long for Ace to be escorted to the other

side of the glass. He was handcuffed and in a prison uniform. He looked haggard and pale, his face more hollow than lean in that dangerous predator type of way. He wasn't having the best recovery from his gunshot wound here in jail.

Good.

When their gazes met, he smiled just like he had back at her cabin, as if he had all the control and power in the world.

She wouldn't let that rattle her. She had the power now. She kept her expression neutral and her posture as relaxed as she could muster. "Hello, Ace."

"Felicity Harrison. This *is* a surprise. My would-be murderer wants to speak to me. I could hardly resist my curiosity."

"You mean the opportunity to try to mess with my mind?"

Ace's smile didn't dim. If anything it deepened so that he looked normal. Like a kind man happy to see someone. Not even a prisoner happy to have a visitor to talk to, but like a man at a family Christmas dinner.

The fact it could look real was far more chilling than him calling her his would-be murderer.

"Care to take a guess as to why I'm here?" she asked. She'd practiced this. Perfected what she would say, how she would broach the topic. Being too direct would give him a kind of ammunition. She didn't know what Ace could still do to her, especially with his impending move to a federal facility, but she wouldn't take any chances.

"So many reasons. But I note you're alone, which

means not one of my sons, and probably not one of your little Knights, knows you're here. They wouldn't let you do this alone."

"I'm not afraid of doing anything alone." It wasn't totally true. She'd told Cecilia. Just in case something happened, though she couldn't think of anything that would. Still, she'd realized that someone needed to know, and Cecilia was the only one who'd be true to her word not to tell anyone unless she needed to.

Ace didn't need to know that. Let him think she was alone. Let him know she could handle it. "I shot you without anyone's help."

"Good. That's good." Ace leaned back and chuckled. "I like you, Felicity. I do." His gaze sharpened. "You don't like that, though. Gage wouldn't be too keen on me liking you, would he?"

Her blood ran cold, but she kept her mouth curved and forced a little laugh out herself. "Yeah, he's that gullible. He'd drop me because *you* said you liked me. And I'm that pathetic, I came here to talk to you about your son."

"Fancy yourself a strong woman now?" Ace's smile got a sharp quality that no one would be fooled into thinking was kind. "You shot me, Felicity. But I'm still here."

"Yeah. Looking a little rough around the edges, though." Felicity leaned forward, trying for his fake kind smile. "Not sure how federal prison is going to agree with you, but I can't wait to find out."

"I can't wait to drag you into a long, painful trial. You and Gage. It'll be a real joy. To taint your lives for years. To always be the dark cloud over your future. To twist and bend the law to my will until I'm walking free again. And when I am—"

It sent a cold shudder through her, but she kept her expression neutral and shoulders relaxed. "The law can be tricky, it's true, and it fails a lot of people."

"When I'm free—"

"But we won't let it fail you. Trust me on that."

Ace yawned, gave an exaggerated stretch. He pushed away from the table in front of him. "Well, if that's all."

She knew she shouldn't blurt it out, but he was standing up. She should let him go. Come back another time. Play his little game, because if she didn't, he'd end up playing her.

But she had to know. She had to.

"My father didn't know about the dead woman."

Ace stood there, smiling like he'd just been crowned the King of England.

Felicity had to swallow at the bile rising in her throat. She'd lost. Already. She should give in and leave.

But she had to know. Mind games or not, she had to know.

Ace sat back down and leaned forward. He clasped his hands together on the little table in front of him and pretended to look thoughtful. "Did you two end up having a little chat?"

She refused to answer.

"Was it tearful? Did your heart just swell right up, being reunited with your daddy?"

She couldn't affect nonchalance, but she could keep her mouth shut, and she did, even if she looked at him with a black fury coating her insides.

"The state never should have taken you away. Is that what you'd like to think? He was misunderstood. It was just the once. He really, truly loves you deep down underneath all his problems."

It stung because once upon a time that *had* been her fantasy. That there'd been a mistake. That her memories were made up. The way Ace said it made it seem so possible.

But she remembered now. That hike in the Badlands, hiding from her father, it had reminded her of a truth she'd known and hadn't wanted.

She knew what her father was.

She just had to know for sure what he'd done. "He said you forced him to help you. He didn't know about the murder. He didn't know what I was talking about."

Ace sat back into his chair, lounged really, rangy and feral even with the sick pallor of his skin.

She'd shot this man and he still held the cards.

"So, you've come in search of the truth," Ace said thoughtfully. "Without my son."

"It's my truth." He wouldn't use it against her. She wouldn't let him.

"He won't see it that way. You and I both know that. Nothing is yours once you're involved with a Wyatt. They fancy themselves better than me, but they're the same. Their name means everything. Their vengeance is all that matters. Every woman they've ever brought into the circle gets swept right up into the

Wyatt drama—don't they? Liza and Nina, your *sisters*, banished because of your boyfriend's brothers."

It wasn't true, but he voiced it so reasonably. Because he believed it. In his warped brain, that was true, and love and duty had nothing to do with it.

Because he had no love, and no duty other than his own evil. It would be sad if he wasn't such a monster.

"My father came to visit you here," Felicity said, keeping her voice bland and steady. She would get to the bottom of things, no matter Ace's tangents. "Before you two showed up at my cabin to enact your little failure. You have a connection."

Ace inclined his head. "He did come. He did indeed. Came to visit. We had a good chat about some things. Then, as fate would have it, Michael was the one who helped me out when the tornado, my divine intervention, set me free. Michael has been a good friend."

"If the tornado was divine intervention, what was that bullet I put in you?" she asked, and didn't try to smile or laugh. She let the disgust—and her win over him—show all over her face.

Ace smiled. "The divine requires payment. Suffering. I didn't become what I am until I had been abandoned, until I suffered and nearly died. This is only my second coming, Felicity. I hope you're prepared."

She shook her head. He struck fear in her and she hadn't come here to be brainwashed. To be made afraid. She'd come here for answers, and that had been stupid. Ace would never give her real answers. Which made her more tired than afraid.

"You know what? Never mind." She had started to

get up, when Ace spoke. Quickly and hurriedly as if, for once, desperate.

"Two possibilities, right, Felicity? One, your father was the bumbling idiot he portrayed himself to be. I used his weakness and stupidity to get to you. He didn't murder his own daughter. It was all me and I framed you both, or at least the people who work for me did. It's a nice story. I know it's one you'd like to believe. But I think you know… I think you know there's another story. Another truth."

She should walk away. He was lying. He had to be lying.

"Once upon a time a man came to visit me. I owed him a favor, from a long time ago. Your father wasn't so much *in* the Sons as he was an associate, one who'd saved me from a particularly bad run-in once. I knew your mother."

She made a sound. Couldn't help it. She knew nothing about her mother, except that she had died. But Ace, this monster, had known her.

"I knew your mother very well."

She almost retched right there.

"But I digress. Your father, excuse me, this *man*, came to see me in jail a few weeks ago. He'd been holding out asking for the favor returned until he really needed it. Apparently, he'd accidentally, or so he said, killed his daughter. He needed an alibi. A sure thing so it never came back to him—murder would certainly put him in jail for the rest of his life. He wanted me to use my Sons influence to make sure that didn't happen."

Felicity absorbed his words. She didn't want the second story to be true, and maybe it was a lie. Ace was nothing if not a liar.

But it made more sense. Unfortunately, the dead body in this scenario, and her connection to Felicity and Michael, made the most sense out of anything.

"Well, I left him to die," Felicity said, knowing her voice wasn't as strong as it had been. "So I suppose it doesn't matter."

"Nightmares never die, little girl. I'm living proof of that. Your father played the fool well, but he was no fool. The truth is, I don't know the truth. I know I didn't kill that girl. Whether she was your sister or not, I don't know. Michael and my resources collaborated to try and make it look like you did it, sure, but you deserved a slap back after getting involved in Wyatt business. As for the murder itself." He held up his hands. "All I know is it didn't have a thing to do with me. So, I guess you'll have to have a conversation with him."

Ace grinned when Felicity said nothing. "Oh, I forgot. He's missing. Very convenient."

"He's dead," Felicity said flatly. She believed that. She did.

Or had. Until talking to Ace.

"That'd be easy, wouldn't it?"

Felicity knew those words would haunt her, and that was her cue to leave. Maybe she didn't have answers, but she'd gotten what she'd come for.

Her father was no hapless pawn of Ace's. But he was dead. Had to be.

GAGE CHUGGED THE bottle of water he'd pulled out of his pack. He wouldn't admit to Brady his head was pounding and that he wished they'd quit two miles ago. Not when he'd been the one to insist on another two miles.

The search for Michael Harrison was fruitless. Worst of it was, he hadn't told Felicity that's what he'd planned on doing today. He didn't want her getting her hopes up. He'd made a good choice there. This was utterly useless.

"Need a break?" Brady asked mildly.

"Nah. We can head back. Rest up. Try again tomorrow."

"I have to sleep sometime. Some of us aren't on desk duty. And you're not coming out here alone. Not until that doctor clears you."

Gage wouldn't be stupid on this, though it was tempting. "I'll see if Tuck or Cody can come with me."

"Be sure that you do. That is, if you make it through the hike back."

"He's got to be out here somewhere," Gage said, using his sleeve to wipe the sweat off his forehead. "Even if he's dead…he didn't just evaporate."

"You've got the winds, animals, caves. Plenty of people disappear without a trace in plenty of places. Especially if they're dead."

"You've always been Mr. Positivity."

"Reality isn't often very positive. You know that, Gage."

Gage followed Brady's path back, scanning the area around them. Not a hint of Michael Harrison where Felicity had left him—or in the miles around where she'd left him, and the worst part was Brady was exactly right.

There were a lot of ways to disappear—dead or alive.

Gage just wanted to give Felicity some piece of closure. It ate at him that he might not ever be able to and that it would weigh on her. Forever.

Gage sighed. Life sucked sometimes. He'd accepted that a long time ago. It was harder to accept for the people you loved, he was coming to find. Growing up, there'd been nothing to do about Ace. Even now there was only so much to be done. He was who he was and his sons were what they were. There was no option of shielding or protecting his brothers—that ship had sailed probably before Gage and Brady had been born.

But finding Michael for Felicity felt doable, and the fact he couldn't do it might drive him crazy.

He could tell when he and Brady got into cell range because both their phones started sounding notifications like crazy.

"That can't be good," Brady said grimly.

Gage pulled his phone out. Ten texts. Five missed calls. Three voice mails. "No. Not good." He opened the texts, read them. Listened to his messages, all variations of the same theme: call me.

What he couldn't figure out was why they were all from Cecilia. She was a tribal police officer on the rez, and spent way more time there than out at the ranch. Of all the Knight girls, Gage had the least to do with her on a personal level, though sometimes their lives intersected on a professional one.

Maybe it was that. Maybe it was something to do with one of her cases on the rez. Relief coursed through him at the solid explanation. "I'll call her, assuming all your messages are from Cecilia."

"Yeah."

He hit Call Back and Cecilia picked up before the first ring had finished sounding. "Gage."

"Hey, Cecilia, what's up?"

"Don't be mad." She sounded breathless and worried, which was the antithesis of Cecilia's usual demeanor—which was either cool as a cucumber or hotheaded as all get-out. Cecilia had no in-between.

His nerves were humming. "Gee, that's a good way to ensure that I'm going to be really, really mad."

"Felicity's missing."

Gage went cold, despite the oppressive heat of the day. "What?"

"She went to visit Ace. I—"

He gripped the phone so hard it was a wonder it didn't crumble. "She did *what*?"

"I can't get it out if you don't listen to me. She went to visit him in jail. That all went fine. But after? She was supposed to call and check in. She didn't. I can't get ahold of her. I already called Tuck, and Jamison for that matter. We've checked in with the jail, and they're working to figure out what happened between leaving the jail and…not coming home. We're handling it, but I knew you'd want to know."

"You're handling it?" He wanted to rage and punch something, but all he could do was grip the phone. "It's hardly handled if she's missing."

"Gage."

"You knew about this. You knew and—"

"I don't have time for you to berate me. She needed to do this," Cecilia snapped. "Alone. And she knew I was the only one who wouldn't—"

"Keep her safe?" Gage replied.

There was an intake of breath and the call ended. Gage swore, but he didn't stop moving. They still had a good quarter of a mile before they got to Brady's truck.

"Well, I heard all that," Brady said grimly, following after Gage. "Felicity's probably back at her cabin. Upset. Visits with Ace are upsetting. She forgot to check in. Took a shower, maybe."

Gage kept walking at the breakneck pace he'd set for himself. "She wouldn't. She just wouldn't." If she told someone, she'd be sure to say she was all right.

Why did she tell Cecilia?

"We should check," Brady insisted.

He had no patience for his brother's calm reason. "No time."

"Don't you think we should be sure before we go anywhere with guns blazing?"

Gage wanted to whirl on his brother and pound some sense into him, but there was no time. Instead, he broke into a jog, no matter how it made his head ache or his stomach roil. "What happened to Nina and Cody after their visit to Ace? They about got themselves killed, but they had each other. She's alone. And she put a bullet in Ace, which means he won't rest…"

Gage swore again. He hadn't fully grasped how much of a target Felicity had made of herself.

All because of him.

He reached the truck and held out his hands for the keys.

Brady had jogged after him, but he stopped resolutely out of reach. "I think I should drive."

"Don't fight me on this."

Brady hesitated, then handed him the keys. "Where are we going?"

"The jail."

Brady winced. "I was afraid of that." But he got in the truck and didn't lodge one complaint when Gage drove like a bat out of hell. Luckily, they'd already been out in Pennington County rather than back at the ranch, where it would take way longer to get to the jail.

Gage parked haphazardly, taking up two spots. He saw Brady eyeing the bad parking job. Gage tossed him the keys. "Here. Fix it. I want to do this alone."

"What exactly?"

"I'll kill him this time. No qualm."

Brady put his hand on Gage's shoulder. "In the jail? Gage. Take a minute. You have to think before you act. Going in there with murder on the brain is a recipe for a whole new disaster we most certainly don't have time for."

Gage shrugged off Brady's hand. "I'll think once we know where she is."

"We know she isn't *here*."

But Ace had to know where she was. What had happened. Why the hell had she thought to do this on her own? Why had Cecilia *let* her?

She should have told him, and he couldn't deal with

the hurt of that when she was God knew where. Gage strode forward, about to wrench open the front door of the jail entrance, badge at the ready, but Tucker stepped out of the door first.

He came up short, looked from Gage to Brady. "Well. You got here fast."

Gage only growled.

Tucker held up his hands. "Listen, we've got a few leads. Her car is still in the lot, so wherever she went, it was with someone else."

"How is Ace doing this?" Brady asked, too much bafflement and not enough fury.

Gage wanted to whirl on him, rage at someone, but it was only the impotent terror building inside of him. He couldn't let it win because it was clouding all rational thought.

"He's not," Tucker said grimly. "At least, it seems really unlikely. The security footage seems to point to a van. No windows. No plates. We've got an APB out."

"And that's not Ace because?"

"Because..." Tucker sighed. "We went over the past few days of security footage, and that van was here every day for the past four, only during visiting hours. No one ever got out. The only time the van moved before the end of visiting hours was today. It moves after Felicity enters the jail. We caught a quick glimpse of the driver. It's not... It's not a clear shot, and there's room for interpretation, but I'm about sixty percent sure the driver is Michael Harrison."

Chapter Nineteen

Felicity had spent the first ten minutes trapped in the back of a van berating herself for her stupidity. She'd been so shaken when she'd walked out of the jail that she'd turned to the sound of her name rather than run from it.

She'd been pushed into the back of the vehicle before she'd had a chance to get her footing. Before she'd had a chance to fight or run or scream—the doors had closed on her.

She was an utterly worthless fool.

The back of the van was completely black. She'd spent most of the drive feeling around, trying to find a handle or some way to get the door open. She could tell the car was going fast because every time it turned she'd tumble around like loose change.

If she could find a door, and open it, she would jump out regardless. Even if he were driving 100 miles per hour. Anything was better than being at her father's mercy.

He was alive. Alive and well from the looks of it. He

certainly hadn't been trapped or lost in the Badlands for the past few days.

The van came to an abrupt stop and she pitched forward, painfully banging her elbow and hip against who knew what.

She didn't let the jarring pain stop her from hurrying back to her feet, crouched and ready. He'd have to open the doors, and he hadn't tied her up or hurt her. Maybe he'd taken her somewhere terrible. Maybe he had a gun.

But she wouldn't go down like she had in that parking lot. Stupid and off guard. No. Absolutely not.

She didn't let herself think about how he'd survived or why he'd come for her. It didn't matter.

She'd fight him no matter what.

He'd taken her purse, and that stung, because she'd been dumb enough to put Cody's little button in there. When Cody had given it to her, he'd told her to wear it on her person. She had, every day, but she hadn't wanted questions about it when she'd been searched at the jail, so she'd put it in her purse before heading inside.

Everything that was happening was because of stupid choices she'd made out of arrogance or ignorance or something. Desperation? Why couldn't she have left it all alone? For her own stupid, pointless conscience.

That line of thought did nothing to help her. She wouldn't let it be the end of her life. She had to be smart. She had to fight her way out of this.

Beating herself up could—and *would*—come later.

The van was still stopped, so she remained crouched

in a fighting position. But when the doors opened, the light was blinding and she winced away from it out of instinct.

Nothing happened as she adjusted to the light. She clenched her fists and blinked as her father came into focus.

He stood outside the van looking grim. "Never could leave well enough alone. You should have let it go, Felicity. Gone back to your life. But you just had to keep poking."

She stayed back in the van, fists clenched as she got used to the light pouring in. "You're the one who dragged me into this. You killed her, and you had me framed."

He sighed. "Ace going to blame it all on me? Typical. But he's in jail and I'm not."

"You killed her," Felicity repeated. She would get his confirmation—if she had been stupid enough to be caught here, she would get his confirmation.

"Yeah, I did. But she had it coming. Did you believe me, Felicity? I ain't killed no one. Oh, I'm so hurt. Don't leave me here to die." He scoffed, not even pleased with himself. Just disgusted. "I'll give you credit for leaving me there to die, but you should have finished off the job if you really wanted me dead."

It dawned on her how much he'd fooled her. Not just about the murder, but about everything. "You weren't hurt."

"Man, you're dumb. Come on out now." He gestured her forward.

The fact he expected her to listen to his directive

made it seem like he, in fact, was the dumb one. She wasn't about to scuttle out there to die just because he told her to.

She stayed where she was, crouched and ready.

"Going to make this harder on yourself." He groaned like an inconvenienced teenager. "Fine. But I warn you, I like a struggle. You won't."

"You'll have to drag me out of here, kicking and screaming," she replied, ready to do whatever it took. He would physically overpower her, no doubt, but she wouldn't make it easy.

He shrugged. "No problem there." He leaned forward, his big body and long arms giving him the reach he needed. She kicked, scratched and bit, but it was no use. He got ahold of her arm and dragged her out. If she landed any blows, he didn't so much as grunt. He jerked her arm so hard and violently she wasn't altogether sure her arm was still in the socket.

Pain radiated through her and for a moment she was too bowled over by it to fight. He dropped her onto the ground, a patch of gravel in front of a run-down trailer.

She tried to breathe through the pain, tried to stand. She managed to get to her knees. He stood over her and reached a hand back, as if he expected her to cower and take the blow.

No. She wasn't a little girl anymore.

She used everything she had to push forward and crash into his knees. Apparently, it was enough of a surprise to knock him backward, and he tripped over the edge of the gravel, sprawling onto his back with a grunt.

She stumbled on top of him. He immediately fought her off, trying to pin her to the ground. He was bigger, but she was faster. She was slithering away when he caught her by the ankle and dragged her back across the hard, painful gravel.

She kicked out, tried to shake off his grasp. He kept pulling her toward the trailer and she knew she couldn't wind up inside. She watched his legs move, timed them and then managed to kick her heel out to strike his ankle. He tripped and lost his grip on her.

She jumped up, knowing she could outrun him. She had to. But before she'd made it three strides, he grabbed her by the shirt.

She'd never grappled with anyone before, let alone someone nearly twice her size, but she didn't let that stop her. She knew the important thing was getting in as many blows as possible. So she punched and kicked and kneed, while his breath wheezed out.

She gave him a nasty blow to the nose, which had blood spurting out. Triumph whirred through her, but it was only a second before his meaty fist connected with the side of her face, sending her sprawling.

Her vision blurred, and her mind seemed to echo in on itself.

Get to your feet. Get to your feet. She could feel her mind telling her to do it, but her limbs took forever to cooperate.

She struggled to her feet again—and she would keep doing so. No matter how many times he knocked her down or got in her way—she would fight.

Fight!

Dizzy and bleeding, pain radiating through her, she stood there ready to fight him off again. There was nowhere to run behind her. It was all rock wall and trailer. But there had to be a way to get past him.

Except Michael didn't come after her again. He leaned into the passenger side of the van and came back out with a gun.

"See, if you didn't fight me, Felicity, you would have avoided this. I didn't want to kill you. Well, not with a gun. It's hard enough getting away with one murder—two would be pushing it." He laughed a little. "But now you're hurt. And you've got my DNA on you, so no wandering in the Badlands till you die for you."

She was woozy and out of it, but she knew one thing for sure. "I'd never have died in the Badlands."

"I'd have made sure of it," he replied, turning the gun on her.

He'd shoot her. No matter what. She could run, but there was nowhere to go that a bullet wouldn't find her. So she wouldn't run. At least not away.

Instead, she ran toward him. If he killed her, at least she'd gone down fighting for her life. At least she'd tried.

She rammed into him just as the shot went off. She didn't feel the piercing pain of a bullet, but the blast of sound next to her ear made it feel as though her head had exploded. She pressed her hands to her ears, trying to somehow ease the horrible sound and pressure.

It was a heck of a lot better than being shot, but the pain was still a shock to her system. Such a shock she couldn't think past the fact she couldn't seem to hear.

Everything was a buzz. She looked around, trying to understand…

Fear gripped her, and in that fear, he won.

He wrenched her arms behind her back. She could feel him tying something around her wrists. The blow must have knocked out more than just her hearing, because it didn't occur to her to fight him off.

She knelt there in the gravel, rocks digging into her knees, hands being tied behind her back and just… prayed.

GAGE TAMPED DOWN the panic. He'd had a lifetime of doing that. Danger had been the story of his first eleven years, and if he was able to survive that, to survive that cave with Ace, he could do it.

His profession had given him the skills to disassociate. To focus on one step at a time to get someone to safety.

He could find Felicity. He would.

He had to.

There had been different sightings of the van, giving different possible directions. Tuck had asked a few deputies to go check Michael's last known place of residence, though no one expected him to be there.

And he wasn't.

Gage had wanted to go, but he knew himself well enough to know his temper wasn't suited for searching. Not for clues. He wanted to be searching for *her*. But he needed a lead, a damn plan.

"We could head back to the Badlands, where she left him," Gage offered to Brady as they drove down a highway someone had claimed to have seen the van driving on. "It's what Ace would do."

"He isn't Ace," Brady replied. "Did you look at his record?"

Gage shook his head. He hadn't given a thought to Michael Harrison other than finding his body so Felicity could rest easily. Quite frankly, when he hadn't been searching for Michael, he'd been headfirst lost in Felicity and what having a normal life with a woman he loved felt like.

"Threats. Assault. Battery. Over and over again. Dude can't control his temper, and thanks to lawyers and judges, never stays behind bars for very long. Which I know isn't exactly a comfort, but I don't think he's enacting the kind of poetic justice Ace is always after. This is just vengeance."

"Why? Felicity didn't do anything to him," Gage returned resolutely. Because if it was just vengeance, she might already be gone. At least with Ace you always knew you had a chance to save someone while he showboated his anointed routine.

"Felicity left him to die and, from what Cecilia said, confronted Ace about his role in that woman's murder." Brady's calm faltered. "He did it. I think Michael killed that poor girl. Not Ace."

"And Ace is innocent?" Gage asked incredulously.

"No. But I think Ace got involved for different reasons, and I think once we've got Felicity back, you'll be able to think the same thing."

"Getting Felicity back is all I care about." Who

cared about the reasons. Who cared about anything except her safety.

He looked out at the highway, analyzing every rare vehicle that passed him by. This was going to drive him slowly insane. Not that he could stand anything that wasn't finding her. If this was all he could do… Well, maybe it'd help him come up with something else.

"You sure you want me to ride shotgun on this?" Brady asked, squinting out the passenger seat window.

Gage blinked at his brother—his twin. "Why wouldn't it be you?"

Brady shrugged. "Because you're mad at me for being calm."

"Any of you would be calm," Gage returned, and though disgust laced his tone, he was glad someone could be. Without Brady and Tucker's calm, he would have already done a hundred stupid things.

"Dev wouldn't be calm," Brady offered.

"I don't need Dev making my worst impulses even worse," Gage muttered, frustrated with the conversation. "I need you, Brady. Ticked off at your calm or not, I need it."

"You got it."

Gage blew out a breath. It didn't ease his fear, but it calmed some of the ragged edges. They were the Wyatt twins. They had a whole army of Wyatts looking for her.

They'd find her. Who knew. Maybe she'd already saved herself. She could face down Ace, surely she could take down Michael.

Gage's phone rang and he answered it tersely.

"Don't get too excited just yet," Cody's voice said without preamble. "But I think I've got a track on her." Gage hadn't heard from Cody this whole time. Gage had figured it was because he was all the way in Bonesteel and not law enforcement in any licensed capacity.

But Cody knew tech and computers.

"Explain," Gage snapped.

"I didn't want to say anything until I was sure it would work. But the button I gave her... Even though she didn't hit it, I'm tracking her. At least the button. If it's on her, I can tell you where she is."

"Then do it." He tossed the phone at Brady, then followed Brady's instructions as to where to drive.

It was a good twenty miles from the jail. Gage didn't let his stomach curdle at the thought of how long she'd been gone, and how little of it would have been in transport.

He focused on action, on reining in his temper. Felicity was in danger. True, mortal danger. He couldn't let his temper be the thing that killed her. "We can't go in guns blazing."

He felt Brady's surprise more than saw it.

"He has her," Gage said, keeping that tight control on his rage, because fear and rage were too dangerous a combination. "We can't risk her. We'll stop here. Go the rest of the way on foot."

Brady nodded. "Stick together until we have our target, then split up if she's not immediately visible."

Since that was exactly what Gage had been thinking, he slowed the truck to a stop. "Ideally, backup is here before we have to engage, but I can't make promises on stopping if she's hurt. I need you not to get in my way. She's too important to me. I need you to understand that."

Brady didn't nod at that. He didn't even agree. But he didn't argue. "Be smart. For both of you—not just her."

Gage flashed a smile he didn't feel. He couldn't promise his brother he wouldn't lay down his life for Felicity. He wouldn't be able to live with himself if he didn't. "We'll see."

Wordlessly they silenced their phones, unholstered their weapons and slid out of the truck. The location of the button was one mile due north. Gage had parked the truck outside a cluster of trees. He and Brady moved forward—two men, one unit, one purpose.

The trailer came into view slowly. It was settled in among thick trees, a rock wall at its back.

Hell of a spot to hide out—but also a hell of a spot to get trapped. Not many ways to escape. The van was parked on a patch of gravel and the back doors were wide open, as was the passenger side door.

It was eerily quiet.

Brady nodded to the right, and Gage gave assent, peeling away to head to the left. If Michael and Felicity were still here, they were in the trailer.

He didn't let himself consider what might have happened if they weren't here.

The windows were covered on the inside with thick curtains, on the outside with dust and grime and a collection of dead bugs.

There was no way to see inside. No way to tell if

they were in there. Gage moved slowly, quietly, gun trained on the trailer. He skirted the side of the trailer, looking and listening for any sign of people.

As he came to the back, Brady appeared from the other side. There was a narrow yard, if one could call it that, between the trailer and the steep rock face. If he and Brady could block both sides, there'd be no way for Michael to escape.

If he was in there. If they could get him out here instead of him running out the front and to the van.

Gage studied the back of the trailer. It was the same situation. The few windows there were covered. The door didn't have any kind of window in it. And everything was quiet.

If they weren't in there, they were somewhere on foot. Unless Michael had another vehicle at his disposal.

Based on this setup, Gage doubted it. They had to be in there. The quiet threatened his ability to stay calm. There was nothing good about quiet—too many awful possibilities.

He wouldn't let himself think about any of them. He crept forward, Brady moving to flank him. Both had their guns drawn and ready for anything.

When shouting from the inside started, Gage gave Brady a look. Brady nodded. Gage eased the storm door open, wincing at the squeak and hoping the shouts covered the sound.

He had one chance. One chance to get in there quick and clean and without putting Felicity at more risk.

He counted to three in his head, then kicked as hard as he could, the door splintering open.

Inside things were dim and dingy, and a metallic smell clung to the air. Felicity was on her knees in the corner. Clearly, her hands were tied behind her. She looked up at him like he was a ghost, but Gage had his eyes on the gun in Michael's hand.

"What is it with you Wyatts?" Michael gave a bit of a shrug, and Gage had been in enough situations to know what that shrug meant. He wasn't going to fight his way out. He was giving up.

But not before he killed everyone he could.

So, Gage pulled the trigger. It was the only thing to do—the only way to save Felicity—he had no doubt about that. Blood bloomed on Michael's dirty T-shirt and he jerked back, crashing into the wall. But his face went hard and he got off his own shot before falling to the ground, the gun clattering out of his grip.

The shot didn't hit Gage, but he heard a crash behind him. "Brady." He whirled.

Brady had fallen, but he was struggling back to his feet, swearing a blue streak as he held his shoulder.

He glared up at Gage. "Get her out of here, damn it."

Brady had been shot. Fresh rage swept through Gage, but if Brady was on his feet it couldn't be all that bad, and they had to get Felicity out. Get all of them out. He rushed forward, putting his arms around Felicity.

"Come on, sweetheart. Can you stand up?"

She struggled to get to her feet, even with his help.

Gage had to work hard to tamp down the impotent fury raging through him.

"I'll untie you when we're outside. Come on, sweetheart. Red, let's move outside."

She didn't move except to shake her head. "I can't hear," she shouted, making him wince as her mouth was close to his ear.

Michael's gunshot must have gone off close to her ears. He bit back a curse and nodded. "Okay. Okay. That's okay. It'll wear off." He tugged her toward the door, giving one look at Michael, who'd gone still.

Good riddance.

Chapter Twenty

By the time the doctors were done with her, she could hear a little bit. If the room was quiet and someone was close enough, speaking slowly. Her ears still rang, and the ibuprofen they'd given her helped her headache but didn't eradicate it completely.

She much preferred thinking about all that than the fact her father was dead, and worse—she'd be dead if it wasn't for Gage.

And Brady, who was currently in the ER having his gunshot patched up.

All because she'd been stupid. She sighed. She kept trying to work up enough blame and guilt to think this was all her fault, but she couldn't muster it. If she went back, she'd do the same. Maybe put up a bit more of a fight in the jail parking lot, but she still would have gone to see Ace, without telling any of the Wyatts.

Would that have changed anything?

It might have changed everything.

But she'd done what she'd done, and she couldn't really hate the result. Except Brady being shot.

She wanted to go home. She wanted Gage. Most of

her life when tragedy had struck, she'd wanted to be alone, to deal in peace and without having to worry if she looked weak or stupid or whatever.

But Gage had showed her that it didn't really matter how you looked, especially when the other person understood. He'd understand the complicated feelings at her father being dead.

She wasn't so sure he'd understand her decision not to tell him she was visiting Ace, but she didn't know how to deal with that, so she just kept pressing forward.

She walked through the hospital, the buzz still in her ears, but she could hear some things. She could understand people if they were close enough and talked directly to her.

The doctors had said the hearing loss would likely wear off, but she had to come back in a week to be checked out again. It had been a relief to know her hearing wasn't irreversibly damaged, but she would have accepted that. Accepted anything over being dead.

She found Gage exactly where she knew he would be, in the waiting room of the ER. She wasn't sure she could accept it if he was angry enough at her to want to end things.

She swallowed. He looked desolate. Pale and lost. But when his gaze moved to her entering the waiting room, he tried to hide that away.

"How's Brady?" she asked.

He spoke in low tones, looking down at his hands.

When he was done, she tapped his arm and then her ear. "Sorry, I didn't catch all that." She slid into the seat next to him.

He shook his head and forced a pathetic smile. "That's okay. He's okay. You're okay." He touched her cheek and slid his palm over her hair. "It's all okay."

She put an arm around his shoulders. "Then why do you look so miserable?"

He shook his head and looked down at his hands for a while, until she tipped his chin toward her so he had to look at her.

"It should have been me," he said simply.

"Why?"

"He wouldn't have been there if it wasn't for me."

"And you wouldn't have been there if it wasn't for me." He gave her a look and opened his mouth to argue, but she shook her head. "You can't play it only the way you like. Either we blame the people who are actually responsible, or you have to blame me."

"Why didn't you tell me?"

It was hurt that chased across his face before he shook his head again and tried to turn away, but she kept a firm grip on his chin. "I should have," she said, hoping her voice sounded as strong as she wanted it to. "I knew you wouldn't like it, so I didn't tell you. I wanted to handle it on my own, thought I had to. Thought you wouldn't let me. But I should have told you. I shouldn't have been… If I was determined to do it, I shouldn't be afraid to tell people. I can't be afraid to disappoint people. If you had been mad at me, I would have dealt with it. I should have told you. Things would be different if I had."

"Well, hell, Felicity, you make it real hard to hold on to a mad."

"You weren't mad. You were hurt." He tried to turn away again, but she wasn't done. "You saved my life. You really did. He was going to kill me. The only reason it took so long was he was trying to find a way to make sure it couldn't be connected back to him. It wouldn't have lasted much longer. He was losing his patience."

He blew out a breath like she'd physically hurt him. "Well, guess we're even, Red."

She swallowed at the lump in her throat. "I'm sorry Ace isn't dead."

"I'm not." He brushed a hand over her hair. "I wouldn't want that on your conscience." He pulled her in, so she leaned on his shoulder.

She wasn't sure it would have weighed all that heavy, certainly not any heavier than him being alive to wreak havoc.

"So, you're not..." Felicity didn't know how to put it. They hadn't been dating in any traditional sense. It had been a relationship, of course, but the words of how to describe anything failed her. Still, she had to be sure. "We're okay?"

It was his turn to take her chin, tip her face up and make her look him in the eye. He brushed his mouth against hers. "You and me, Red? We'll always be okay. One way or another."

She wouldn't cry at that, though she wanted to. So, she looked away. "Where is everyone?"

"Brady told me not to call anyone. Said he was fine and—"

Felicity made a noise of outrage. "What! They're

going to hear it through your cop grapevines? I don't think so. If you don't call them, I will."

"You can't hear well enough to make a phone call."

"We'll see about that." She made a move to grab her phone, then realized her purse was still somewhere in her father's van. Dead father. She shuddered. It was necessary, but that didn't mean she'd have the images from today out of her head anytime soon.

Gage handed her his. "Here you go, tough girl."

She took it primly, then wrote a text because Gage was right—trying to talk to anyone on the phone would be difficult.

When she handed it back to him, he was just staring at her. So serious. Everything inside of her jittered with nerves.

"I love you. It would have killed me, just killed me, if he'd hurt you. And I can't promise you that Ace will never come after you again. Worse, I think if we're together, that'll make it more… He'll take it as a challenge to hurt us. All the ways he can. I don't know how to live with that."

She reached out and pressed her palm to his cheek. She'd known he was a good man, but she thought he didn't have that core of nobleness that Jamison and Brady had, which was often more annoying than impressive. Like this was. "You'll have to find a way, because I love you, too, and I'm not going to be shaken off that easy. Ace can try to hurt us."

"Feli—"

"No. You don't have a choice. Quite literally. I won't live my life afraid of Ace. Neither will you. If he tries to hurt us again, we'll fight again. Together. So, just shut up."

He managed a chuckle. "All right. Sounds good."

"Good." She let out a breath and leaned against him. "You're probably going to have to marry me, too, but we can talk about that later."

She felt him stiffen underneath her, but it made her smile. It'd give him something to be anxious about besides his brother and trying to protect her, so that was good.

A nurse came in and smiled kindly. "Gage. You can go back and see your brother now." Felicity stood, too. "I'm afraid you'll have to stay out here, ma'am."

Gage gave her arm a squeeze. "By the way I'm telling him it's your fault when everyone shows up."

"That's just fine."

Since he still looked haunted, she reached up on her toes and brushed her mouth against his. "It's over, and it's okay." She was ready to believe it.

BRADY WAS LAID out in a bed. He was pale, but at least he looked pissed. It took energy to be pissed.

"Hey. How's it going?" Gage asked lamely, hanging by the door rather than stepping farther inside.

"You know, I'm a trained paramedic. I know a thing or two about medicine. You think any of these doctors or nurses will listen to me?" Brady grumbled.

"So, it's true. Medical professionals really are the worst patients."

Brady grunted as he eyed Gage. "I'm not going to

shout all the way over there to have a conversation with you, and you can leave the guilt right there. I'm fine."

"You won't be able to work for weeks."

Brady pulled a face, but then he lifted his uninjured arm. "It happens. It's what we risk every day we work, isn't it?"

"It wasn't work. You didn't have to be there."

"Where else would I be?" Brady shook his head. "Reverse it, Gage. Where would you have been?"

Much as he didn't want to admit it, he would have been right behind Brady. Always.

"I don't think you realize what you did," Brady said, once Gage got closer to the hospital bed.

"Let you get shot?"

"Gage. You stepped in front of me. We both saw what Michael was going to do. We've both been there before. The only reason I couldn't get off a shot, too, was because you'd stepped in front of me, blocked me. Damn stupid. But that's what you did. The only reason I got shot was because…well, bad luck really. Your shot got off first and his aim was off."

"I don't—"

"Maybe it's not how you remember it, because you were focused on Felicity, but that's what you did. I'm not going to argue about it. I'm tired and my shoulder hurts and they keep wanting to pump me full of medicine I don't want. So, if you can't get over it, get out."

Get over it, maybe not. But he could set it aside.

"It isn't like you to play martyr," Brady said with no small amount of disgust.

"I'm not—"

"And since it's me, why don't you just say what you're really all wound up about."

Because it was Brady, it was hard to pretend he wasn't right on the money. "I guess I know what she felt like after she left Michael to die. I thought I did. I did, in a way, but not like this. I know I did the right thing."

"There's not a doubt in my mind he would have killed her."

"Mine, either. Or hers. But, Brady, if this was all Michael, those charges don't get used against Ace."

"Ace tried to kill you. Himself, not through some two-bit lackey. You can testify to that. Even if we can't get him on murder, he'll go to a higher security prison for attempted murder."

"If he doesn't, Felicity is in even more danger."

"Then I guess you're pretty lucky to have each other's backs, huh?"

Gage didn't know if he'd go so far as *lucky*, but it was certainly a blessing to have…this. His brothers, his family. Everyone would rally around and protect. It was what they did.

"We know how this goes, I think. He took a swing at Jamison, then Cody. It doesn't work, then he moves to the next. If he finds a way to go after one of us again, it's probably not going to be Felicity."

Gage looked at the bandage on Brady's shoulder. They left it unsaid, but it was pretty clear that if Ace found a way to manipulate the system again, Brady would be the next target. He was weakened.

"He said he had a list. A list and I'd messed it up. I wasn't supposed to be next. Which means, we could—"

Brady shook his head. "I'm not here to out-manipulate Ace. If we ever beat him, really beat him, it won't be using his own tactics."

Gage looked down at his hands. "Growing up, Ace told me I was smart, and could take his place, so I did a lot to prove I wasn't and couldn't. He told you you were stupid and weak, so you did a lot to prove you weren't." Gage had never believed he was his father, though sometimes he'd been afraid he could have inherited his impulses. But he fought them and that was all that mattered. He'd never considered that his father might have stamped him in different ways. "Did he shape us?"

"Are we running the Sons? Come on, Gage. If he shaped us, if he left a mark on us, it only got us here. We help people. You saved Felicity. Whatever he did, didn't work. We're the good guys."

Gage looked up at his brother, pale but alive and irritable. He smiled a little. "Felicity saved me first."

Brady chuckled, then winced. "Your ego can take the hit."

Gage studied his twin. "Thank you," he said, letting the words have the weight they deserved. Brady opened his mouth, and Gage had no doubt it was to argue. He shook his head. "You were there. It means something. Thank you."

"Fine. You're welcome. Now leave me alone."

Gage nodded, headed back to the door. He stopped there, knowing exactly what Brady needed. "Oh, by the way, Felicity notified the cavalry, so expect some visitors."

Brady swore and Gage laughed. It felt good to laugh, though it died when he reached the waiting room and Cecilia was standing there with Felicity.

She was still wearing her tribal police uniform. When she saw him, she squared her shoulders and lifted her chin, like she was ready for a fight.

"I came to—" she made a face like she was forced to swallow something bitter "—apologize."

"Don't."

Cecilia frowned, looking at Felicity. "That's what she said, too."

Gage smiled at Felicity. It was good to be on the same page, to understand without discussing. He turned back to Cecilia. "If you thought she'd be in danger, if either of you thought that, I know it would have been different. We all know if she *hadn't* told you, and you hadn't told us right away things weren't right, everything would be different." He swallowed at the horror that tried to get through, but it hadn't happened. "We can't change anything. We just have to… Look, this takes away the charges against Ace. And…"

Felicity slipped her hand into his. "It just means we have to look out for each other. Together. And we agree no more trying to do things on our own. Not when it comes to Ace."

Cecilia didn't say anything to that.

"You want to go in and see him?" Gage asked, nodding back toward the door he'd just come out of.

"Uh. Well. I mean, I guess," Cecilia replied, looking uncharacteristically unsure.

"I'm going to take this one home. She needs some rest."

Cecilia nodded. "You both do."

Gage gave Felicity's hand a squeeze and they headed for the exit. Felicity looked back at Cecilia, who was straightening her shoulders again, all soldier ready to go into battle.

"What?" Gage asked.

"I don't know." She tilted her face toward him and smiled. "Just…should be interesting."

"What should be interesting?"

She laughed as they walked out of the hospital, into daylight and freedom and hope. "You'll see."

Epilogue

Trials weren't fun, even when you won. It had been grueling days of testimony—including Felicity's own and Gage's. On the stand she'd had to relive shooting Ace, and she wasn't particularly thrilled about it.

Especially with what else was twisting inside of her, uncertain and scary and huge.

But it was over now, Ace guilty of too many charges to count and being moved to a higher security prison much farther away.

It was relief, even if it wasn't full closure. They walked out of the courthouse, a group of four Wyatt boys and three Knight foster girls who'd survived Ace's influence. Out into a sunny day that felt completely right.

Gage's hand slid over hers. Her stomach jittered with new nerves, because now that the trial was over she couldn't ignore her suspicions. And she could hardly not tell him.

Still, she smiled easily and exchanged hugs and goodbyes with her sisters. They shared something now, and even without that, Felicity had come to understand some things about growing up the way they had that made it easy to forgive Liza and Nina their choices to leave. And embrace their decisions to come back.

Gage said his goodbyes and gave Brady a gentle hug. He'd had a setback with his gunshot wound, an infection, that had left him on desk duty for way longer than any Wyatt should have to endure.

Still, she liked to think the trial's outcome had taken a bit of a weight off his irritation.

She and Gage went to Gage's truck and slid in. He would drive her home, and spend the night in her cabin, but he'd be gone before she woke up—to get back to Valiant County and his job.

Her stomach jittered more. Things would have to be different. She hadn't figured out a way that would make them both happy.

"Nothing quite like testifying together, right?"

She forced a smile. "Better than doing it alone, I think."

"You think right," Gage said, patting her knee as he pulled out onto the highway.

Gage chattered the whole way home, and though Felicity tried to keep up, she was caught in her own loop of thoughts and worries and what she had to do.

Gage pulled to a stop in front of her cabin and she quickly slid out, afraid if they dawdled she'd blurt it out.

It needed more finesse, and she should be sure.

But Gage was right behind her, his arm around her

waist as she walked up to the door. "All right. What's up, Red? Something's freaking you out, and it's not the trial. Tucker himself is going to oversee the jail transport. Ace won't—"

"I think I'm pregnant." She closed her eyes as the words fell out. Flopped there in between them as they stood awkwardly on her front stoop.

He didn't say anything. Didn't move. And she just stood there with her eyes squeezed shut, not having a clue what to do.

She'd tried to plan it out, tried to know what else to say and how to handle his reaction, but she always reached this point and then shut down. She could only wait, eyes closed and panic keeping her frozen.

"I guess it's a good thing I applied for the opening at Rapid City."

Her eyes flew open. "What?"

"Rapid City is hiring. I was tired of being that far, and you could hardly leave your dream job."

"But you work with your brothers, and now..."

"And now, God willing, I'll get the position, and we'll be in the same county and...and..." He inhaled sharply. "You sure?"

"No." She shook her head a little too emphatically. "I bought a test, but I didn't want to take it until the trial was over. I should have taken it first. I just had to tell you."

"Well, hell, go take it," he said, all but pushing her toward the door.

She nodded. Her keys shook in her hands, but she finally opened door and went into the bathroom to take the test. She went through the motions, set the timer on her phone and then let Gage into the bathroom.

"We have to wait three minutes."

"Okay." He swallowed, looking down at her, but the concern and worry in his expression slowly changed into something else. Then he pressed his mouth to hers in a gentle, calming kiss. "I love you, Felicity."

"I know, but before we know for sure, I don't want you to feel like… Duke isn't going to hold a shotgun on you. I mean, he might, but you don't have to marry—"

"I applied for that job for a reason, Felicity. Yeah, to be closer, but because I wanted to start getting things situated for the future. And maybe I was waiting for a little kick in the butt—but here it is. I was getting there before this."

"This is faster."

"Yeah. But I think we can do it." He lifted her hand and pressed a kiss to it. "I *know* we can do it. And so do you."

The timer on her phone went off and they both jumped.

"Okay." She *did* know they could do it, but it helped to hear. Helped to be steadied by someone else. She took a deep breath and looked at the test sitting there.

"Translate for me," Gage said, his voice a bit strangled. "What does two lines mean?"

"Pregnant," Felicity said, staring at the results window, where there were two lines clear as day.

"Pregnant," he repeated. Then he laughed and lifted her clear up off the floor, still laughing. Happy.

"You're happy," she murmured, because he was a constant marvel. She knew they were good together, knew he'd want to do the right thing, but she wasn't sure he'd jump right to happy.

"Yeah, hell of a thing, but yeah." He put her back down on her own feet. "Are you happy?"

Since her throat was clogged with tears, she could only nod and rest her forehead on his chest. *Happy* didn't seem a big enough word. But there was reality, too.

"He might get out some day. That trial wasn't the end. God knows he'll appeal. Ace touching our lives isn't over."

"Maybe not," Gage agreed.

It was scary, especially with this new life growing inside of her, but he was holding her. They were in this together. She lifted her head and looked up at him. "But we'll have even more to fight for, right?" She put her hand over her stomach. It was impossible to believe something was there—a life. Impossible to fully grasp, and yet true.

And right. So right.

"We have everything to fight for," Gage agreed, sliding his own hand over hers. "And we already have, so we know we can again." He pulled her close, tucked her hair behind her ears. "So, you going to marry me? Before the baby, just in case Duke gets any ideas about making me disappear."

She tried to say yes, but her throat was too tight

with tears. And hope. And joy. So, she nodded, and he kissed her until she thought her knees might dissolve.

"It's going to be a good life," he said, a promise and a vow.

"Yeah, yeah, it is."

* * * * *

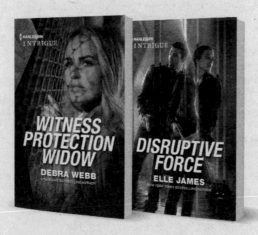

Prologue

They warned him not to go to the police.

He couldn't think. Couldn't breathe.

Forcing one foot in front of the other, he tried to ignore the gut-wrenching pain at the base of his skull where the kidnapper had slammed him into his kitchen floor and knocked him unconscious. Owen. Olivia. They were out there. Alone. Scared. He hadn't been strong enough to protect them, but he wasn't going to stop trying to find them. Not until he got them back.

A wave of dizziness tilted the world on its axis, and he collided with a wooden street pole. Shoulder-length hair blocked his vision as he fought to regain balance. He'd woken up a little less than fifteen minutes ago, started chasing after the taillights of the SUV as it'd sped down the unpaved road leading into town. He could still taste the dirt in his mouth. They couldn't have gotten far. Someone had to have seen something…

Humidity settled deep into his lungs despite the dropping temperatures, sweat beading at his temples as he pushed himself upright. Moonlight beamed down on him, exhaustion pulling at every muscle in his body, but he had to keep going. He had to find his kids. They were all he had left. All that mattered.

Colorless worn mom-and-pop stores lining the town's main street blurred in his vision.

A small group of teenagers—at least what looked like teenagers—gathered around a single point on the sidewalk ahead. The kidnapper had sped into town from his property just on the outskirts, and there were only so many roads that would get the bastard out. Maybe someone in the group could point him in the right direction. He latched on to a kid brushing past him by the collar. "Did you see a black SUV speed through here?"

The boy—sixteen, seventeen—shook his head and pulled away. "Get off me, man."

The echo of voices pierced through the ringing in his ears as the circle of teens closed in on itself in front of Sevierville's oldest hardware store. His lungs burned with shallow breaths as he searched the streets from his position in the middle of the sidewalk. Someone had to have seen something. Anything. He needed—

"She's bleeding!" a girl said. "Someone call for an ambulance!"

The hairs on the back of his neck stood on end. Someone had been hurt? Pushing through the circle of onlookers, he caught sight of pink pajama pants and bright purple toenails. He surrendered to the panic as recognition flared. His heart threatened to burst straight out of his chest as he lunged for the unconscious six-year-old girl sprawled across the pavement. Pain shot through his knees as he scooped her into his arms. "Olivia!"

New York Times bestselling author
KAREN HARPER'S

new trilogy is set in rugged Lost Lake, Alaska, about a woman desperate to flee her toxic past and the wilderness survival tracker whose devoted protection heals her shattered heart. Perfect for fans of compelling romantic suspense in the vein of Heather Graham, Kat Martin and Carla Neggers.

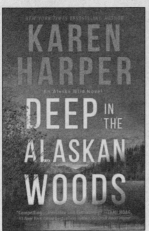

The first in a new trilogy by Karen Harper, *Deep in the Alaskan Woods* follows Alex Collister as she flees an abusive relationship to live with cousins who own a B and B in Lost Lake, Alaska. There she meets wilderness tracker Quinn Mantell. The two are instantly attracted to one another, but Alex fears getting close to another man after her last relationship ended so catastrophically. But when suspicious scratches are found leading up to Alex's window, and a Lost Lake resident is found dead with similar scratches on her body, Alex enlists Quinn's tracking expertise to help her circumvent the danger. His protective instincts make her realize that some men are worth trusting. But if she gives him her heart, will they survive long enough to fall in love?

Coming soon from MIRA books.

Love Harlequin romance?

DISCOVER.

Be the first to find out about promotions,
news and exclusive content!

 Facebook.com/HarlequinBooks

 Twitter.com/HarlequinBooks

 Instagram.com/HarlequinBooks

 Pinterest.com/HarlequinBooks

ReaderService.com

EXPLORE.

Sign up for the Harlequin e-newsletter and
download a free book from any series at
TryHarlequin.com

CONNECT.

Join our Harlequin community to
share your thoughts and connect
with other romance readers!
Facebook.com/groups/HarlequinConnection

HSOCIAL2020